THE

WIDOW MORTIMER;

OR,

THE MARRIAGE IN THE DARK.

A Romance.

BY THE AUTHOR OF "THE STRING OF PEARLS," &c., &c.

London:

PUBLISHED BY E. LLOYD, SALISBURY SQUARE, FLEET STREET.

WIDOW MORTIMER.
𝔄 Romance.

BY THE AUTHOR OF "THE STRING OF PEARLS," &c., &c.

CHAPTER I.

SHOWS WHAT THE PRINCE OF WALES SAID AND DID AT THE WHEATSHEAF.

 OUSE—house—house! Hilloa—house, I say. What the deuce, are you all asleep, and only one in the morning? House—house, I say. Open doors, and draw corks! Hilloa—hilloa! House—house!"

This vociferous appeal was made at the door of the Wheatsheaf, at Pimlico, at one o'clock in the morning of the 24th of June, *Anno Domini* 1796; and the party who created such a disturbance was a man of small—but not particularly so—stature, with a rubicund face, indicative of good living, while three others at a short distance appeared to be wonderfully enjoying the fun.

"House—house—house, I say. Open doors, and draw corks."

"What is all this noise about?" cried a voice from an upper window. "What do you mean by it, you drunken reprobates? Be off with you, or I'll call the watch."

"Will you, really?" said he who had been kicking at the door. "If you do, the watchman will be so dazzled by your beauty that he will not be able to see what he is about, and will take himself into custody instead of us. Oh! what eyes you have, Maria."

No. 1.

"Go it, Sherry. Go it," said one of the little party, who was only a few paces off. "If that don't move her, nothing will in this world, I'm sure."

"Go away, go away," said the damsel who had appeared at the window, but she spoke in a much milder tone of voice,—"go away, I say, in peace. You can't come in at this time of night.'

"Ah, Maria, you are the prettiest barmaid in London. What a figure—what cheeks—lips—what——"

"Oh! I know you now, you reprobate," said the girl. "You are Mr. Sheridan."

"Stuff! I'm no such thing."

"Who are you, then?"

"Devilish dry, my angel; and if you don't come down and open the door, I and my friends here will be under the disagreeable necessity of kicking it down, for in we will come, by some means or another. There's a slight rain falling upon me, though my friend is standing under a doorway, because his *reign* has not begun."

"Sherry, Sherry, mind what you are about. I don't exactly choose to effect an entrance to the Wheatsheaf by a declaration of who I am. Be careful, there's a time for all things, Sherry."

"Oh, there's no danger. In we must get, somehow or another; what say you, Hill?"

"Break the door down, to be sure."

"Here goes, then."

"Gentlemen, gentlemen," said Maria, "I would, under ordinary circumstances, let you in; but you must know that Mrs. Mortimer was married to-day, and——"

A roar of laughter from the whole party drowned the conclusion of Maria's speech, and such was the noise that several windows were opened in the street; and one testy old gentleman, who lived exactly opposite, succeeded in throwing a jug of water upon the party, which was anything but agreeable.

"Damn it!" cried one, "this is not comfortable. I say, Sherry, we are drenched. This sort of thing won't do, you know. It's no use battering at that door; if they won't open it, they won't."

"Oh, but they will, though."

"Watch—watch—watch!" cried an old lady, from the window of a house a few doors off. "Watch—watch."

"The plot thickens," said Sherry. "Maria, Maria, will you see your adorer dragged to the watch-house?"

The girl had disappeared from the window, and just as the sound of a watchman's rattle came upon the ears of the invading party, the public-house door was opened, and the barmaid said,—

"Come in, then, if you must; but let me implore you to behave yourselves like gentlemen, or I shall have all the blame of it. Come in, do, and don't stand there waiting till the watchman comes."

The party, consisting of four individuals, darted into the house, and they only succeeded in doing so just in time, for several watchmen reached the spot the minute after, and looked about in vain for some one upon whom they could revenge themselves for rousing them from the comfortable repose they were all having in their various boxes.

Maria, the pretty barmaid of the Wheatsheaf, showed her guests—who probably, she shrewdly suspected, would pay her well for her trouble—into what was called the bar-parlour, where, rather boisterously, they sat down, and asked for wine.

This she supplied them with, and although it was none of the choicest, they had already had enough to make them not over scrupulous with regard to quantity, or very capable of distinguishing good from bad; so they drank it without any deprecatory remark.

"Come, Maria," said one, a stout, fair young man, with a heavy physiognomy, and sleepy-looking eyes, "tell us all about it. Did you not say that your mistress was married to-day?"

"Indeed she was, sir; to Mr Booker, a very respectable man, indeed."

"Oh, no doubt—no doubt," said Sherry, "of course, he's a very respectable man. But, Maria, I have a slight reminiscence that I heard something of your mistress being married last year."

"Oh, yes, sir, she was. That was to Mr. Green, the retired chandler of Bond-street, you know, sir, but he died."

"Oh, then this is Mrs. What's-her-name's third marriage, I think, for she was a widow before that, I'm sure, and always called Widow Mortimer."

"Why, gentlemen," said the girl, as she lowered her voice, and glanced suspiciously round, "between you and me, you must know it's missus's sixth marriage; but she always calls herself Widow Mortimer again, when her husband dies, because the house is well known as Widow Mortimer's; and she thinks it might hurt the business to have another name put up.'

"The devil! Her sixth marriage, did you say, Maria, or are you only joking?"

"Not at all, sir—it's no joke, but the honest truth, as sure as I is here, and a Christian girl, gentlemen. But you won't say I told you?"

"Oh, no, no, no!"

"Well, then, there was Mr. Lee, Mr. Luton, Mr. Fiddler, Mr. Brown, Mr. Green, and Mr. Booker."

"Well, but that's six, and she calls herself Mortimer besides, so that there may have been seven."

"Goodness gracious! yes, gentlemen, as you say. Isn't it dreadful to think of? and Mr. Booker is such a very quiet, inoffensive-looking man. He is a retired builder, you see, gentlemen, who used to come here of an evening to enjoy himself and smoke his pipe, and, like everybody else, he was taken with the widow."

"True," said he who was called by his companions Sherry, "and, to tell the honest truth, she is a charming woman. I only regret that you won't have an opportunity of seeing her to-night."

These last words were addressed to the stout, fair, young man, who replied, laughingly,—

"Oh, never mind; another time will do as well, Sherry."

"Perfectly; she will, no doubt, soon be a widow again. Maria, what, in Heaven's name, becomes of all the husbands—eh, my girl?"

"They go off, sir, like snuffs of candles—a sort of consumption, the doctors say it is; but there's no such thing as saving of 'em, and it's as good as a picture to see the attention she pays 'em."

"But you know, Maria, there are some very bad pictures."

"Oh, of course; but she is very attentive, for all that, and behaves herself just as she ought to do; and all I can say is, that she must be a very strong-minded woman to go through so much."

"That she may be," said Sherry; "but what sort of a strong mind must the man have who ventures to make Widow Mortimer his wife? But you need not sit up, Maria. We will remain a short time where we are, and when we go, we will pull the street door after us very slowly and carefully, and there's a guinea for the wine and the trouble you have had."

"Thank you, gentlemen; but the fact is, I hadn't gone to sleep, you see, when you knocked, nor, indeed, had I gone to bed, for I had only just reached my room. We have all been in such a bustle to-day, on account of missus's marriage; so I'll stay in the bar, and then, if you want anything, you can let me know, if you please, gentlemen."

"Very good, very good; you are a kind, good girl, Maria, and shan't lose by it.'

Maria, no doubt, knew her customers pretty well, or at nearly two o'clock in the morning, as it then was, she would not have been quite so complaisant as she was to them. As it was, he walked out of the room, leaving them with lights and a couple of bottles of port before them, into which they had already made a considerable inroad.

"Now," said Sherry, when they were alone, "now, if we don't have some fun in this house, it will go hard with us, I think. Here we are, and a married couple up stairs. What do you propose, Hill, eh?"

"Well, upon my life I hardly know, unless we get out on the top of the house, and find out which is the chimney of their room, and throw wine bottles down it."

"Or all of us creep into the room," said another, "and get under the bed, and hoist it up suddenly, so as to tumble them both out."

"Or rush in," said the fair young man, "and all of us roll over the bed, and the amorous couple screaming like so many fiends let loose."

"Ingenious, gentlemen, very," said Sherry. "Now, I propose that we get a lot of sheets or table-cloths, and, wrapping them round us, go and personate the ghosts of Mrs. Mortimer's departed husbands. We can all stand round the bed, and groan, you know, dreadfully; and if that don't kick up a row, I don't know, from my soul, what will."

"Agreed, agreed! and we can do what we all propose afterwards, for the matter of that."

"So we can, so we can! Good God, what's that?"

CHAPTER II.

INTRODUCES THE SOMNAMBULIST, AND SHOWS THAT SOMEBODY HAS A DISTURBED CONSCIENCE.

THE hasty exclamation with which we found it necessary to close our last chapter was uttered by Sherry, as the door of the bar-parlour, exactly opposite to which he was sitting, suddenly opened, and a figure appeared, which certainly was calculated to excite both surprise and alarm.

It was a woman of tall and commanding form, attired in a night-dress of most exquisite whiteness, which was likewise profusely trimmed with rich lace. The cap she wore was of the most costly description, and but partially confined the ringlets of glossy auburn hair, which, in some instances, had struggled from their confinement, and fell, rather in pleasing relief of colour, upon the snow-white dress that she wore.

It was not positively the fact of the appearance of a woman, and that a handsome one, in a rich and costly night-dress, that would have struck them with amazement and likewise some degree of terror, but it was the strange and unnatural appearance of the woman.

Her eyes were fixed and glaringly wide open, and yet there was " no speculation" in them, and it was quite evident she did not see any one who was present. She moved along, too, with a strange gliding and stealthy footstep, which was more like that which might have been attributed to some supernatural agent than any living, breathing human being.

And so she made her way into the bar-parlour.

"What's this, Sherry?" said the stout, fair, young man. "I say, Sherry, damn it, what's this, eh ?"

"Hush ! a somnambulist."

"A sleep-walker ? The devil ! don't let her come near me."

"Hush ! she speaks. Let's listen. It's Mrs. Mortimer, of the quire of husbands."

Slowly the sleep-walker crept onwards, carefully avoiding the furniture that was in her way, and yet appearing to do so by some species of instinct, for she certainly did not look at the chairs, she stepped round so cleverly; and as she went, she slowly rubbed her hands together, and spoke in a low voice,—

"It's only a pang of a moment. The corner bureau. Three drops are enough. Hush, hush ! How the wind howls. Time enough—time enough. £20,000 will do it—yes. The corner bureau. Three drops—only three drops. Hush, hush, hush !"

"Wake her— for God's sake, wake her."

"No, George, no," said Sherry, "let her be ; it's devilish interesting—upon my life, it is. Let her be, I tell you, and get out of her way ; we will see what she will do next."

"Yes, three drops—only three. The corner bureau. Three drops—hush, hush ! of course he will do it if I wish it. All is well—well—well—well."

There was in one corner of the room an antique-looking bureau, and towards this the sleep-walker made her way slowly, but surely. It was locked, and she made vain attempts to open it, muttering to herself, as she did so, strange words, indicative of a desire to get something from it ; and then moaning when she found that it resisted all her efforts to open it.

At this moment, Maria, who was rather surprised at the sudden suspension of the rather noise commotion of the guests, came to know the cause ; and the moment she saw her mistress in the room, and so attired, and the rather scared looks of the company, she said,—

"Oh, gracious, how horrid ! She is beginning to walk in her sleep again."

"Has she done so before ?" asked Sherry.

"Oh, yes, yes. I have had to watch her many a time, and she does say such strange things, it's quite horrible to hear her, poor thing ; and she always goes to the corner bureau."

"But what will she do, when she finds it locked ?"

"She will go back again quietly enough, if you do not wake her up. But if you touch her, she will scream the house down, and be very ill. Oh, gentlemen, for God's sake, let her be, and she will soon go back again quietly to her bed-room. I'm all of a tremble when this happens, and ill myself for a week after."

"I don't wonder at ——'

Mrs. Mortimer, or rather Mrs. Booker, as she ought to be now called, sobbed piteously for a few moments, when she found she could not open the bureau; and then muttering still the words, "Only three drops, only three drops," she turned, and slowly made her way towards the door of the bar-parlour, and left that apartment.

It was quite a relief to every one present when she was gone, but she scarcely had left above a moment, when Sherry jumped up, and taking a candle from the table, said,—

"I must see the end of it."

"What would you do," said Maria. "You have seen all there is to see : you would not follow her into her bed-room, surely, would you, sir ? And she will go there,"

"No—no, only to the door, Maria. Only to the door, and you may come with me if you like."

"Don't go, don't go," said one.

"Pshaw ! nonsense, who knows but I may be able to bring all this in with wonderful effect on the stage, you dogs. You know I have an eye to business, though everybody says I never had any such thing.

As he spoke, he walked through the door-way, closely followed by Maria, who begged most earnestly to him in a low tone of voice to stop, and not follow her mistress any further, who, if she heard of it, would be most mortally and seriously offended with her, Maria, for permitting him to do so."

"You can tell her you couldn't help it, you know," said Sherry, "and that will have all the novelty of being truth from a barmaid."

It was indeed quite useless for Maria to attempt to stop him, and he followed at a few paces' distance from Mrs. Booker, who walked with a strange apparition-like step along a passage, and finally up the principal staircase of the public-house, towards the second-floor, where the sleeping chambers were situated.

It was a large, old-fashioned rambling-house. It was pulled down when Buckingham Palace was built, and it had not been originally intended for a public-house; so that in and about its ancient rooms, there were decorative fixtures, which time had certainly dealt harshly by, but which, for all that, sufficiently proclaimed what the place once had been.

Truly the old place was like some faded beauty. There was abundant evidence yet that there had been charms, although they no longer were charming, except to the lovers of antiquity.

It was a much larger house than was at all required for the present business that was carried on in it; but as it was got for the rent of a small establishment, there was no objection to it upon that score. The old balustrades of the staircase were of mahogany, which, in some places, had been richly carved; and here and there was supported by some gilt iron work, the gloss of the gold upon which was entirely gone, although there could be no doubt of its once existing. On the second-floor, was a large landing, and a kind of corridor from which branched seven bedrooms, some two or three of which were of great extent, and would, if properly appointed, have been of great beauty; but the furniture then in them was but of an ill-assorted character, being either the cheap and shabby, or the cheap and old, with dilapidations incidental by the progress of time.

Mrs. Booker paused on this landing, and then turned to the left and went towards a door, on the panels of which was a quantity of carving or raised wreathes of flowers, possibly in some sort of composition; and above which was a large representation of the arms of some noble family, possibly, in times gone past, proprietors of the mansion which had now so sadly degenerated as to become a public-house.

"Oh, Mr. S——, Mr. S——" said Maria, in an agitated whisper, "she is going to the haunted room."

"The what?"

"The haunted room, sir. I wouldn't set foot in it after midnight, or, indeed, after dark, for all the money in the Royal Mint, that I wouldn't, sir. No, not to be made a duchess."

"A haunted chamber, and a sleep-walking landlady with an unlimited stock of husbands," said Sherry. "Upon my word, I had no idea that the Wheatsheaf had so many attractions; and, by-the-by, among them last, though not least, I ought to number the prettiest barmaid in London, ay, or out of it."

"Oh, sir!"

"Truth, upon my honour. That is a subject upon which I never joke. But what is your mistress about?"

"Going into the haunted room, as you are a sinner."

"I subscribe to both propositions. I will follow her into the haunted room, taking an opportunity afterwards to prove your own opinion of yourself, Maria. A most gloomy-looking place upon my life, I feel a sort of all-overishness already; and this is veritably a haunted chamber, is it? What's that, a bed? or—or—what the devil——"

Mrs. Booker uttered a loud shriek, and fell upon the threshold of the door of the haunted chamber, while Sherry at the moment fancied he saw something flit across the haunted chamber.

Her own cry awoke the somnambulist.

The house was now in a state of great confusion, for the scream that the landlady had uttered was really of that terrific character, that for anybody to attempt to sleep upon it was ridiculous. It must, without the interposition of any prince whatever, have at once awakened the sleeping beauty in the wood, long before her lease of a hundred years repose was expired. No wonder, then, that it reached the ears of Sherry's companions below, and that it still more roused up Mr. Booker, who up to this moment had been sleeping in a state of perfect unconsciousness of the loss of his better half.

The three companions of Sherry rushed up from below, and the highly respectable Mr. Booker made his appearance in his night shirt, looking very much scared, and wondering what it was all about.

Maria had lifted up her mistress, and dragged her away from the threshold of the haunted room, the door of which was closed; and now the landlady looked about her with a countenance expressive of the greatest alarm, and shook from top to toe, as if she had been in the last desperate stage of ague.

"Never mind, ma'am," said Maria; "you have only been walking a little in your sleep, ma'am; you know you have done it before, so you need not be alarmed. Here's Mrs. Spittikins, the cook, coming, ma'am, and between us we will help you to bed again."

This was done, and Mrs. Booker was led off. Sherry gave Booker, who stood looking the picture of surprise and consternation as if rooted to the spot, a violent blow on the back, as he said,—

"Well, old fellow, how do you feel?"

"Not very well, thank you. What's it all about? That was my wife, wasn't it?"

A roar of laughter followed this question; and he, whom they called George, said,—

"Yes, Booker. She's a vampire, or something of that sort. You will have to tie her down in the bed to prevent her going off to some churchyard to eat up the dead, while you are in the arms of Morpheus."

"The arms of who?" said Booker.

"Be off with you to bed, man, can't you, at once. You have only married a woman who is given to gadding in her sleep. Now, I am going to be married soon, and I should like nothing better than for my wife to get up, and be off somewhere. What say you, Sherry?"

"Why, that's something near the fact, I suppose. But let's go, and finish our bottle. Come along—come along. We shall soon be off now, Maria, my love."

"Why, she aint here," said George; "you see double, already. Come away with you at once. I have had quite a dose of all this. Come on, I have some broiled bones in the Haymarket,—we know where to get them."

"Agreed, agreed. But once let me be put on the scent of a mystery, and if I don't follow it up, my name isn't——. Well, well, we shall see. we shall see. The haunted room, and the landlady with the unlimited supply of husbands, have both charms for me. By-the-by, Booker must be a bold man, don't you think, Hill?"

"Oh, very—very."

With peals of laughter, for all the pathos of the landlady's appearance as a sleep-walker was soon forgotten by those lighthearted spirits, they left the Wheatsheaf and its inhabitants to repose.

The clock struck three.

CHAPTER III.

SHOWS HOW MR. BOOKER GOT UNEASY, AND ASKED HIS NIECE AMELIA TO COME TO THE WHEATSHEAF.

"My dear," said Mr. Booker, as he and his wife, the landlady of the Wheatsheaf, sat at breakfast, on the morning after the occurrences we have related, "my dear, how are you this morning after your sleep-walking, eh? I hope you didn't take cold."

"Cold," she replied, "why, Anastasius Alfred, how could you think I was to take cold in the house. Be easy about me, my love, and attend to your own health. You have looked poorly for the last month or more."

"Indeed, you never told me that, Mrs. Mortimer."

"My dear B——, how can you call me Mortimer? My last husband, Mr. Green, never made that mistake, even so soon as the morning after his marriage. But it's no matter, love. Is the tea to your liking, duck?"

"Oh, yes, but——"

"And will you take another slice of the Cumberland ham? Do you know, my dear, I always fancy the hams from Cumberland to be the finest flavour of all. It was poor dear Fiddler got me into the habit of taking a slice for breakfast."

"Fid—Fiddler—Green! Why, who was Fiddler, and who was Green?"

"They were two of my former husbands."

Mr. Booker dropped his knife and fork, and gasped again, as he added faintly, and with a strange gurgling sound in his throat,—

"And—and who was Mortimer?"

"Only another. Mortimer was a friend of Brown's, you see, my dear, which enabled me to know him; and since you put on looks of surprise, my love, allow me to ask if you were not aware how many times I had been married before? Surely you must have heard."

"No, no, never—upon my soul. How many times in round numbers, eh—my—dear?"

"You are my seventh. I am glad of the opportunity myself of telling you, for the fact is, you might possibly have heard it from more ill-natured lips than mine, you know; and now that you do know it, you cannot feel otherwise, of course, than quite easy and satisfied. Why, you are better already, duck. How delightful is mutual confidence, is it not?"

"Very," said Booker, with a groan, "oh, very. But who is this?"

"Oh, it's Mr. Proudfoot, my man of business. Good morning to you, sir. Pray sit down if you please, sir. How uncommonly well you are looking, to be sure, Mr. Proudfoot."

"Thank you, madam, thank you," said the lawyer, who was a most sinister-looking personage, ' thank you, madam, I am pretty well, though not so young as I was twenty years ago. I believe I attend here at your special request, Mrs. Booker, in order to execute a legal instrument, which shall place Mr. Booker in complete and unreserved possession of all your property, in case it should please Providence to take you all to himself, my dear madam."

"Which," said Booker, abstractedly, "would make the eighth."

"Sir?"

"Oh, nothing, nothing. Don't mind me, Mr. a—a—Proudfoot. Don't mind me. I was thinking of Providence took Mrs. Booker, Providence would have a—a—a—you see Providence would be—you understand."

"Perfectly, sir; nothing could be clearer, nor more vividly expressed."

"Exactly; you are a sensible man, sir. But I was not at all aware of this business you say you came about."

"No, my dear, I dare say you were not," said the widow. "I have no doubt you were not aware of it; but the fact is you made a settlement of a very generous character when we married, and which left, as before, my own means entirely under my own control; but I was resolved to show you that I could likewise be generous, and I now intend making a will, which leaves all to you in case of my death; for how true it is, that ' in the midst of life we are in death,' and who shall calculate upon prolonged existence?"

"That's true enough; but yet, my dear——"

"Nay, Mr. Booker, I anticipated you would make objections to this; but I am quite resolved. Have you, Mr. Proudfoot, the necessary documents with you?"

"I have, madam."

"Then, I have made up my mind, and am quite ready to sign them, and two of the servants of the house can be witnesses to the affair."

"Admirable, admirable," said the lawyer; and then he whispered to Mr. Booker, "Quite a woman of business, aint she?"

"Yes," said Booker, "she's done the business of six already."

"What did you say, my dear?"

"Nothing, my love!"

"I thought you spoke, my darling duck."

"No, my chickabiddy."

"How delightful," said the lawyer. "Cooing and billing—actually cooing and billing. And now, Mr. Booker, perhaps you will be rather surprised to hear that Mrs. Booker is worth £12,000."

"Indeed! I am surprised. You don't mean that surely? Why—why—I understood you had a few hundreds only?"

"Well," said his wife, with a smile, " £12,000 is not many hundreds after all; and when I am gone, you can enjoy all that I have, you know. May you be happy with it, and that you may is my most earnest prayer."

"Well, my dear, I cannot help saying that this is exceedingly generous and great conduct of you, especially as you were aware that all I had in the world was a life annuity of £300 per annum, and so I have it not, you see, Mr. Proudfoot, in my power to emulate the generosity of my wife, for I have nothing to leave."

"Never mind," said Mrs. Booker, with an enchanting smile, " you will never think that my affection is other than of the most disinterested character."

"That he cannot, madam," said the lawyer, "and yet—bless me what a thought——"

"What—what?" cried Booker.

"What an idea! Well, upon my word and professional reputation—why, Mr. B—, you can make just such a settlement as your wife is making."

"I—I—you jest."

"No, I never jest—never. The law is a serious business. But I tell you you can, and it's what I call a most charming idea—oh, delightful!"

"What do you mean, Mr. Proudfoot?" cried Mrs. Booker. "How wrong of you to keep us in such suspense."

"Well, madam, I will explain myself. You will be charmed, Mr. B——, you really will. I will point out to you how you can draw your wife's ten or twelve thousand pounds at her death, if you like, or anybody else you please. Of course, Mrs. B——, you keep up the establishment so that Mr. B—— is put to no expense."

"Mr. Booker can draw what money he likes of my banker, for any purpose. Of course, my dear, you know that, don't you?"

"Well, well; but the plan—the scheme, Mr. What's-your-name? How are you going to enable me to leave any one any such sum as you mention?"

"Easy enough. You have nothing particularly the matter with you, I suppose?"

"Certainly not—nothing at all."

"Then, sir, your yearly income will just about pay the premium on life policies, for about ten or twelve thousand pounds on your life, and that's the way you can do it. What do you think of that?"

"Why, it——"

"Didn't strike you before, did it now? I knew what you would say. You will do it at once, of course, and duly make over and assign the policies to your wife, who then will see that you have imitated her in generosity."

"Well, I see no objection."

"To be sure not."

Mrs. Booker burst into tears.

This settled the matter, and Mr. B——, when he saw how deeply affected she was, quite forgot the six previous husbands, and, as he kissed away the pearly drops, he said,—

"My dear, you don't know how happy it makes me to be able to show you how I esteem you. I will insure my life at once. What if it uses up my whole income, I shall be a dependant only upon you?"

"No, no," said Mrs. Booker, "this must not be; you mistake me, Booker; I wept at the bare possibility of losing you, and I say it must not be; do not think of it."

"Oh, but I——"

"Hush!" whispered the lawyer, "say no more about it; but meet me at my chambers, in Gray's Inn, in two hours hence."

"Agreed."

"Let it drop," added Mrs. Booker. "Say no more to me on so disheartening a theme, I beg of you."

"Very well, my dear, I won't—I won't. Then dry your eyes. Come—come, we will say no more about it. Good morning, Mr. Proudfoot."

"Good morning; and long may you both enjoy the happiness of each other's congenial society. Good morning."

Mr. Proudfoot went away without having got Mr. Booker to execute the deed he came about. But poor Mr. Booker was in such a state of confusion that he did not think of that; and when, in about an hour and a half, he sallied forth to go to Gray's Inn, he scarcely knew whether he stood upon his head or his heels.

He certainly had a confused notion that he was going to do a wonderfully noble act which would comfortably use up all his income, and that was all.

CHAPTER IV.

A NIGHT IN THE HAUNTED CHAMBER AT THE WHEATSHEAF.

THE conversation of the noisy little party who left the Wheatsheaf, after Mrs. Booker's somhambulistic feat, naturally turned upon the occurrences of the evening there.

He whom the other called Sherry seemed to be most particularly struck with the adventure, and at times, indeed, he was quite thoughtful about it, which was such an unusual frame of mind for him to be in, that he was subjected to most unmerciful raillery from the others for indulging in it.

"Well, well," he said, "rail on and laugh as much as you like, I am of Mat Prior's opinion, that

"'Care to our coffin adds a nail no doubt,
While every grin so merry draws one out;'

"so laugh and grow fat; but for all that, I am very much struck by what we have heard to-night."

"In what way?" said the stout, fair young man, whom they called George; "in what way?

I only regret that we did not manage to get on top of the house as was suggested, and throw quart bottles down the chimney of Booker's bedroom."

"Well, gentlemen, I have made up my mind," said Sherry, " to know more of it. There is a mystery, that is quite clear; and it's the haunted chamber that seizes upon my fancy. I did not think there was such a thing to be had even in London, where they say you may have anything you like for money."

"And so you may," said Hill, "and so you may; if your fancy lie in the way of haunted chambers, you have only to advertise for a few."

" Ah, but I want the genuine article—the natural production, not an artificial one; and it seems to me that I have found it at the Wheatsheaf."

" And what do you mean to do?"

"Pass a night in that haunted room, which, although all of you laugh at, none of you would do."

There was great merriment at this determination, and as by this time the party had arrived at the house in the Haymarket, where they had announced their intention of going, they entered it rather in a boisterous and riotous manner. Some expostulation was about to be made by the proprietor of this night house; but when he advanced and looked at his guests, he all at once

No. 2.

became wonderfully complaisant, and said nothing about the noise, but ushered them into an apartment where they could be at their ease.

It is no part of our intention to follow the mad vagaries of these bloods upon town, as they considered themselves to be. In the first place, it would be, as it were, travelling out of our record so to do, as our story more concerns Widow Mortimer than such persons; for the second we should find some trouble in adapting the doings of a parcel of mad caps and licentious young men to our pages.

The reader may therefore imagine that the remainder of the night was passed in every possible description of excess, and please to accompany us towards dusk on the next evening to the Wheatsheaf.

Maria was alone in the bar, when he who was called Sherry came in.

"How now, my darling?" he said. "All alone?"

"Yes, sir; this is not a time of the day at which we do much business, and so I have a few minutes to myself, not that they last long enough to give me a positive rest; for, really, there's no such slavery as being in a public-house."

"I can imagine that, my dear. I ought to know something of public-houses, for I think I have been into every one in London; but, Maria, I want to ask you some questions."

"Some of your jokes, I suppose, sir."

"Not at all, if for only once in my life, and for the novelty of the thing, I assure you, Maria, I am quite serious."

"Well, then, sir, I am anxious to know what you have to say."

"It's this, Maria: my curiosity has been very much excited by what you told me about the haunted room that is in the house, and I want you to manage so that I shall pass a night in it."

"You, sir,—in the haunted room?"

"Precisely; it's my fancy, and I am sure you are too much a friend of mine, and know I have too many uses for a couple of ghosts, to baulk me. I assure you, I mean no trick, Maria; it's a genuine wish to pass a night in a room reputed to be haunted, that's all. I want to know what sensations one has. Can you manage it?"

"Oh, it's easy enough to be managed; but——"

"But what? Can there be any reason against it, Maria? What harm now can result to you or any one?"

"Well, well, sir, as I say it can be easily enough managed—of course I don't see any harm in it. I only know that I wouldn't sleep there for worlds, and if you continue in the same mind, you had better come in and regularly take a bed for the night; and then, when you want to retire, I can easily show you into the haunted room instead of the one that is prepared for you."

"Admirably arranged—most admirably, Maria; you are a perfect Talleyrand in private life—the Machiaville of the public trade; you are, indeed. I'll be here at ten precisely, and mind secrecy—no mention to any one of what is doing; for, although I don't mean any trick myself, I don't want to be the victim of one on the part of another."

"You may rely upon me, sir; and as for the two guineas——"

"They are here."

"Many thanks, sir, many thanks, you shall not be disappointed, you may depend; but it's a funny idea, though, of course, there's no accounting for tastes, you know."

"Except in one instance, and that is the universal admiration that is bestowed upon you, Maria. That is fully and completely accounted for by your charms of face and figure. What eyes, what cheeks, what a waist, what a foot, what an ankle—what——"

"Go along with you, will you, I won't listen to you. Oh, you are a deceitful man; anybody may see that in your looks."

Sherry laughed and walked away, but he was true to his appointment at ten o'clock, and strolling into the public-house, he said to Maria, whose mistress was within hearing,—

"Can I have a bed here to-night?"

"Yes, sir. Walk into the parlour, if you please, and it shall be ordered to be got ready for you."

This was so much in the natural order of business, that Mrs. Booker (late Widow Mortimer) paid no sort of attention to it, and the bed was got ready, being in one of the rooms opening from the long, old-fashioned corridor before mentioned.

Mr. Booker was not at home, and as he had gone to pay a visit to an acquaintance in the neighbourhood, who was an old widower, and as he made some statements to that acquaintance which gives us some information, we may as well listen to him.

"I begin to feel wretched," he said, "for I have found out that my wife has already buried six husbands."

"Oh, pho!" said his friend, "it's perhaps not true—all calumny. Who told you any such nonsense?"

"Why, I had it from tolerably good authority, namely, herself."

"The deuce you did!"

"Yes, she told me I was the seventh. Now, what would you do under such circumstances? I am very wretched; really, I could almost get into the round pond in the park, I feel so miserable. The idea, you know, of being the seventh! Isn't it dreadful and overpowering? Oh, my friend Thompson, what can have become of the other six? That's the dreadful and harrowing question I put to myself."

"Buried, of course."

"Yes, I suppose so. It don't want a conjurer to tell me that, but it's odd, aint it very odd! A sort of cold shiver comes over me when I think of it, and the blood don't circulate in my veins properly. Oh, Thompson, I am undone!"

"Do yourself up again, then," said Thompson. "There's no help for it now, you know; make the best of it. What's done, can't be undone. Make the best of a bad bargain. Go home and sit in the bar and drink away at brandy-and-water till all is blue."

"Heigh-ho!" said Booker, as he rose. "I shall not survive it long, I have been to-day to take the first step towards insuring my life for £12,000. And I shall send for my niece, Amelia, who is an orphan, poor thing, from the country, now that I have got a sort of home for her, and perhaps having one of my own kindred about me will console me in some measure. What do you think?"

"That it's a very good plan, if your wife will let you."

"Let me? Oh, she is very kind in all respects, and tells me to consult my own wishes in everything. I have nothing certainly to complain of in that respect, to give the devil his due. Oh no, I can't say one word against her temper hitherto, and she means to leave me all she possesses when she dies, if she should go first. Good-bye, I told her I would be back to tea."

"Good-bye, old fellow, keep up your heart—never say die. Now there was Mrs. T——"

"There, there, you have told me all about that, you know, at least twenty times before, so spare yourself the trouble."

"Ah," said Thompson to himself, "the temper of Booker is not what it used to be. Oh no. I rather think he has put his foot in it. Well, well, I am a widower, and if once I get caught again, damn me! Ha, ha! I am a widower, as jolly as possible!—much jollier than a bachelor, because I know what's what, and have no foolish hankering after matrimony! Ha, ha, ha! a jolly widower!"

Mr. Thompson lit a very elaborate and curious amber-tipped pipe, and mixing himself a glass of tolerably potent grog, he sat down with that bland smile upon his countenance which may be supposed to rest upon the face of a man who does not care how the world wags, and who considers himself a mere spectator of the great, busy, bustling riot of existence that is going on around him. What a truly delightful state of things, if any poor, fretted, tortured devil, who has to struggle and fight his way in this world, could bring his affairs to it—elysium itself!

* * * * * * *

"Now, sir," said Maria, at eleven o'clock, to Sherry, "the bedroom is all ready, if you please, sir, I think you said eleven."

"You are quite right," replied Sherry, and he spoke in a subdued and sober tone, for he knew that Mrs. Booker was in hearing, "you are quite right, young woman; I wish to get to bed early. I will follow you if you will be so good as to show me which way I am to go."

Maria carried the light, and preceded Sherry, and when they came to the landing from whence the various chambers of the house opened, she pointed to one, saying,—"That is the room to which I was to show you, and if you are wise, you will go there now, and sleep quietly, instead of tempting the ghost in the haunted room."

"Why, my dear," he replied, "if it's a female ghost, I will tempt it. I have so often tempted the living, that I should feel some curiosity in tempting the dead."

"Oh, how can you talk in such a manner? you quite terrify me. There, then, if you will go, take the candle, and be off with you. I shall be up all night, so that if there's any alarm, you can ring for help, you know."

"And you will come?"

"Certainly not. I will call the pot-boy."

"Oh, d——n the potboy."

Maria ran down the stairs, laughing; and Sherry, after a few moments pause, opened the door of the haunted chamber, passed in, and carefully closed it behind him again, fastening a little bolt which was under the lock, and which made it impossible for any one to get in without his knowledge and cognisance.

It certainly was a curious room, and from its size and the many ornaments that were about its walls and ceiling, it must have been, at one time, the principal chamber in the house. Indeed, the carved arms above its door, on the outside, marked it out as enjoying, or rather as having enjoyed, at one time, that distinction. The chimney-piece was quite a work of art, and of enormous size, and the walls and roof were divided into compartments, in each of which were raised wreaths of flowers, which, when fresh from the hands of the artists who had designed them, must have had a remarkably rich and fine effect. The room was furnished, and the carpet upon the floor was soft to the foot, while in one corner was a huge ancient bedstead, the hangings of which were dark and sombre, and at the corners of which were plumes of feathers somewhat similar to those which now are placed upon a hearse.

Some arm-chairs were here and there, and a table was near to the fire-place.

"Well," said Sherry, who held up the light and looked about him, "it aint a very nice place now, whatever it may have been. I won't lay down, for I have a peculiar horror of a damp bed, but I will sit in one of these old chairs for a few hours, and see what becomes of it.

As he glanced towards the old grate, it was a great satisfaction to him to see that a fire was laid, and only wanted to be set light to, which he at once did, but the wood was so damp and the coals so cold and moist, that he was some time before he could coax up a flame, which, however, he at last succeeded in doing, by dint of vigorous fanning with his hat. When once the wood was fairly alight, the chimney gave evidence of having a capital draught, for the wind roared up it like a furnace, and a cheerful fire soon cast its ruddy glow to the various articles within that ancient room.

"This is something like comfort now," he said, as he drew a chair close to the fire and rubbed his hands. "It can't want more than half an hour to twelve, and any sensible ghost comes at twelve, of course, or he or she don't come at all upon this occasion."

The fire light so completely overpowered the candle that he thought it prudent to put out the latter in case he might want it when the coals began to get exhausted, as he had no fresh supply, and accordingly he did so; and every now and then he glanced over his shoulder, fancying he heard something, and beginning to feel some of those strange and vague sensations of superstition which no human being is quite free of."

"How a real ghost would take at the Lane," he muttered. "We should have a crowded house every night to a certainty. Ah, that would be an attraction, to be sure. Eh? what was that?"

He thought he heard a slight noise; but he was not quite sure; nevertheless, as it seemed to come from the direction of the bed, he lit the candle again, and went there to look.

There seemed to be everything necessary for repose upon the bed, but sheets; but there was nothing at all of an alarming character, and he looked under the bedstead with some curiosity, but all was vacant. There was a quantity of dust, and that was all. Then he thought he would make a careful examination of the walls in order quite to satisfy himself that there was no other entrance to the room, and found nothing of the sort, so far as he was able to discover.

"Oh," he said, as he sat down, "I dare say the difference of temperature made in the room by the fire has made the old, damp bedstead crack a little."

There was no poker; so with his foot he crushed down the fire, which was beginning to burn very hollow, and once more a cheerful enlivening blaze shot up the chimney.

"I dare say now," he soliloquised as he sat down again, "I dare say the prince and the other blades are having a good laugh at me for my romance in undertaking this adventure. Well, well, I took a strange fancy to it, and I am not in the habit of baulking myself of my fancies because anybody may laugh—not I; I do wish, though, that I had taken the precaution to order Maria to place a couple of bottles of Madeira in this room; but I suppose if I had she would not have crossed the threshold to do so."

He sat now for some time in silence, watching the flames as they burst from out the coals in little jets of pure white flame, of great freedom and intensity; and then, as the supply of gas became weaker, and more mixed with deteriorating vapours, those flames became yellow and red, until they died away entirely. The coals were rapidly consuming, and huge cavernous-looking chasms began to appear in the fire.

But still it lent a ruddy and warm comfortable-looking glow to the room, and the warmth was most decidedly acceptable, although the weather was mild and serene enough, but yet that room, so long closed, with its dismal, antique, damp furniture, would indeed have been wretched without a ————

Hush! The clocks in the neighbourhood strike twelve; yes, the midnight has commenced, and if the supernatural world has any terrors, now is the time when, by the almost universal consent of mankind, it is supposed to exhibit them to the appalled eyes of humanity.

CHAPTER V.

DETAILS WHAT SHERIDAN SAW IN THE HAUNTED ROOM.

YES, it was twelve. Sheridan heard that it was twelve; and as he counted the strokes that proclaimed that hour, a strange, chilly sensation came over him, despite the fire close to which he was, and he felt one of those strong presentiments that something unusual was going to happen, which few persons who have lived long enough in this world to experience its varied sensations have altogether avoided.

A strange, half-stifling and yet very cold air appeared to fill the room. He thought of making an appeal to the bell, but when he strove to move from the chair on which he sat, it seemed to him as if he had no more power than a babe, and as if all his physical energies were as completely in abeyance as in one paralysed.

Affairs were growing certainly serious.

He would by all means now have rung the bell, if he could, for he did not at all like the physical blight that had come over him; moreover, his imagination began to be very much excited as regarded what such a state of things could portend, or end in.

About ten minutes he thought had elapsed after the sound of the neighbouring church clock's striking twelve had come so plainly and distinctly upon his ear, when the fire shot up a small flickering kind of flame, and he seized the opportunity to cast a hurried glance round the room, in order to see if he really were alone, and that there were not present with him some of the strange shapes of another world, whose being there caused the suspending chill in the atmosphere, and, likewise, the odd sensations he felt.

No, there was nothing alarming in the room—no hideous spectre form met his eyes—all was quiet. He saw no grinning demoniac visage laughing at him from between the curtains of the bed, although it would not have been at all surprising if his imagination had pictured such to him.

He felt a little reassured, and was about making a great effort to attend to the fire, when he happened to cast his eyes upon one of the old-fashioned, faded arm-chairs that were in the room, which stood on the other side of the fire-place, exactly in the situation that the other stood which he occupied.

It was no longer vacant!

With bated breath, and a heart beating at a terrible rate, while for a moment a kind of mist seemed to come over his eyes, he glared at the chair, and made out by the fire light that it was a respectable-looking man who was there seated, and who had nothing at all terrible in his aspect.

True, his apparel was not of the most modern fashion, and the face was very pale, but beyond that, there was nothing exactly to lead to the idea that he was otherwise than human, except the singular circumstances under which he was then seen.

Terror, certainly, for a time froze up the faculties of Sheridan, but a sort of devil-may-care spirit that he possessed, began gradually to exert its influence, and he overcame the first emotions which this supernatural visitor had awakened in his mind.

He tried to rise, to satisfy himself that he was not being cheated—that no trick was being played off upon him—for that was what he suspected—but, somehow, he could not move. He felt as if held down in the chair by a hand of iron, and at this his alarm slightly increased, but not sufficiently to overpower all sense; and he made up his mind that come what would of his so doing, he would speak to the apparition, and ascertain, if possible, what brought it there, and who it represented, with its pale face and serious aspect.

But when he tried to speak, his tongue almost clove to the roof of his mouth, and he could hardly utter a sound that was articulate. From what followed, however, it would seem that the ghost understood him; and the succeeding matter for the short space that suffices to describe the events of t' at strange night is taken from a memorandum left by Sheridan among his papers.

"Who and what are you? Speak, if you can," said Sheridan.

The lips of the spectre did not move, but a voice said,—

"Mr. Sheridan, I am John Mortimer's spirit. I died in this room this night eleven years since."

"John Mortimer?"

"Yes, the first husband of her who now calls herself Mrs. Booker, God avenge my murder!"

"Well, but—don't ye?——He is gone No, no. Yet—yet this is not he! Another—another. Why, good God, sir, who are you?"

There was sitting in the chair a little, thin, meagre-faced-looking man, with grey hair, dressed in a suit of snuff-colour, with large buckles on his knees and on his shoes.

"My name, Mr. Sheridan, in life," he said, "was Mr. Thomas Jephson Lee. I was Mrs. Mortimer's second husband. God avenge my murder!"

"This is horrible," cried Sheridan. "Stop, stop, I beseech you. Tell me more."

"He who follows will do so. My mission is over when I say, 'Beware of a slip of the knife.'"

The form of the little old man faded away; and as the perspiration rolled down the face of Sheridan—for who would not be moved at such a scene?—he saw a bulky-looking, gentlemanly man in the chair, to whom he said, faintly,—

"Sir, who are you?"

"Mr. Septimus Luton, sir. God avenge my murder!"

"But—but——"

"And beware of the simulated affections of one who kills while binding up a wound from the slipping of a knife. Beware! beware!"

"For God's sake, Mr. Luton, stay, and——He is gone. I shall go man—or I am mad! Help! help! My voice sinks to a whisper. What is the meaning of all this? Oh! horror! horror! Here is another! and there will be yet—another! I shall die—die."

The chair was filled again by a long, thin young man, with a vapid expression of countenance, and, in faltering accents, Sheridan asked,—

"Who are you?"

"I am Benjamin Fiddler, done to death by Mrs. Mortimer. God avenge my murder! Never let your wounds be stanched by a rag on which three drops have been placed. Death! death! Oh, death! He who comes will tell you more. I must be away—away—away."

The figure slowly faded from the chair, but ere the last vestige of its dim outline had passed away, there came another.

This was a man in much more modern costume than any of the others. He looked awfully ghastly and horrible; there was a white foam about his lips, and he seemed to shake. By this time Sheridan was so terribly cut up by the succession of spectres that he did not speak, and the apparition was equally silent. Then they sat glancing at each other.

At length, after this ominous silence continuing for some time, Sheridan remembered that he had often heard it asserted by believers in supernatural visitants, that they cannot speak unless first addressed by mortal lips. He had often laughed at and ridiculed such superstitions; but what was he now to think? With a feeling of desperation, he said,—

"Will you declare yourself to me? Who are you?"

"My name is Brown. I was husband to Mrs. Mortimer. God avenge my murder."

"Tell me more—tell me more."

"The knife slipped, and seeming affection stanched the wound. The pure current of the blood was poisoned. I can say no more; but question him who will follow me."

"I—will—I—will," gasped Sheridan.

The apparition glided away, and was succeeded by another, who looked like some one enduring the very extreme of agony; and his eyes were fixed upon Sheridan, with such a look of imploring pity, it was enough to move any one to tears to see them.

"Let me ask of you," he said, "information which others have denied me. Who and what are you? and were you, too, murdered? and, if so, tell me how the foul deed was done."

"Listen," said the spectre. "It is my mission to tell all. My name is Green; I was the last husband of the Widow Mortimer, as she called herself, before she contracted the present alliance. God avenge my murder!"

Sheridan, when he heard these words, was afraid that this spectre, like the others, was about to vanish without saying anything more satisfying upon the subject, and he cried,—

"Oh, stay; I implore you, in the name of Heaven, to stay, and to be explicit in your revelations."

"I am abjured," said the spectre, "and I speak. Let him who calls Mrs. Mortimer 'wife,' beware of the bureau, and three drops from the violet bottle, compounded by Gervase, the French quack. Beware—oh, beware. Murder—murder—murder!"

"Stay, oh stay."

"My time has come. The knife slipped—my time has come."

The figure slowly faded away from his sight, and the chair was empty. Sheridan felt as if the spell which had hitherto held him down to the seat was taken off him, and he sprang to his feet with a loud cry.

To reach the bell-pull was the work of a moment, and he rang a peal which soon aroused the whole household, at the same time that he cried aloud,—

"Help, help, help! Lights, lights, lights!"

There was a rushing of feet, and a slamming of doors; and then there came a blaze of light, as Maria opened the door of the haunted chamber, and just looked in, with a candle in her hand. Close behind her was the pot-boy, and in another moment Mr. Booker appeared, and two persons who had been in the parlour below, and upon whom at twelve o'clock the doors of the public-house had been shut, to allow them to finish some mixed liquor they were consuming. Such a crowd of persons completely blocked up the doorway, and as they all spoke at once, it was difficult to understand what they exactly said; but Sheridan advanced towards them, saying,—

" Clear away, for God's sake, and let me leave this room. Clear away, clear away.'

" But how come you here ?" said Booker.

" My good sir, who are you ?"

" My name is Booker, and I——"

" Am the last husband of Mrs. Mortimer. By God, sir, I wish you joy, and if you want any information about your predecessors, just shut yourself up in this room at midnight, and place an empty chair opposite to you, that's all."

" The man's mad," cried Mrs. Booker, suddenly forcing herself through the throng. " What do you want here ? Who are you, sir ?"

" Madam, I want nothing at all, and I am your very humble servant," said Sheridan. " I have passed some time in that haunted room, and I don't think I shall ever want to pass any more in it, or even in this house."

" The fool has had a dream," said Mrs. Booker, with an expression of great contempt; " but how came he in that room at all, Maria? I think I really ought to send for a constable and give him into custody."

" Why, ma'am," said Maria, " I don't know anything about it. I showed the gentleman to the bed he took about ten o'clock in the evening, if you recollect, ma'am; and as to how he got into the haunted chamber, how can I tell, ma'am ?"

" Oh, I shall have a constable. Here, you Bob, fetch a constable directly. My dear," turning to Booker, " you will, as the master of a public-house, you know, have to be made a constable."

" If you will allow me to state, madam, how I came into that room, I think you will not want a constable."

" Well, sir, how ?"

" Why, the fact is, I sometimes walk in my sleep, and I suppose I did so now, and fancied I wanted three drops of something out of a bureau. You understand, Mrs. Booker."

Mrs. Booker started back, and trod upon the toes of one of the guests; she turned of a death-like paleness, and could not evidently command her power of speech for a few moments. When she did, it was to say,—

" If any one knows you, sir, and that you are a respectable man, and your design not likely to be robbery, I have no sort of objection to let you go."

" I know the gentleman, ma'am," said Maria; " he is a first-rate gentleman, ma'am, and a friend of the prince."

" Then he may go."

" Sir," said Booker, " I am sorry you have been troubled at all. I suppose you are, like my wife, given to bad dreams. I have only been two nights married, and you may take my word for it, sir, that——"

" Mr. Booker," screamed the landlady, " what do you mean by talking in that highly inde-corous way? Do you want to put me in my grave, Mr. Booker?"

" No, my dear, I was only saying——"

" Then don't say it, sir."

" Ladies and gentlemen,' said Sheridan, " I have the honour of bidding you all good night. I shall go and sleep elsewhere, if it's all the same to you; and, Booker, I'm sorry for you, upon my soul. You look a decent sort of fellow."

" What do you mean, sir ?" said Booker.

" I can say no more; but I tell you, if you want any information of a highly gratifying cha-racter, you have only to keep watch and ward in that room from eleven o'clock at night until one in the morning. Do it, Booker, do it, I advise you strongly."

" A madman! a madman!" said Mrs. Booker. " It will be a good thing when the house clear of him. Who knows but he may kill somebody. Get out of the house directly."

" With pleasure, madam. Good night ! Good night !"

CHAPTER VI.

MR. BOOKER'S NIECE AMELIA COMES HOME, AND FINDS A LOVER TURNED A SOLDIER.

THE following letter was written by Mr. Booker to a Mrs. Wizzlepan, in Shropshire, who had the care of Miss Amelia Booker, his niece.

"The Wheatsheaf Tavern, Pimlico, London, July, 1796.

"MY DEAR MADAM,—The remittances that I have been able to send you from time to time, for the use of my niece Amelia, I am gratified to hear have always come safe to hand; but I write this letter to tell you that you will be soon freed from your charge.

"You are aware that Amelia is the only child of my poor sister Anne, who died in your house, and whose husband, as you are well aware, was too much addicted to the bottle to make a good mate for anybody; and, taking all things into consideration, it's really quite as well he is in another world as not. But, to come to the point, my dear madam, I have to inform you, that I am married, and as I have now a home of my own, to which I can with propriety invite Amelia, I here do so, and hope she will be as happy in London as she has been with you. I here inclose a five-pound note for necessary expenses, and with best remembrance and best thanks for past favours, believe me to be, my dear madam,   Yours faithfully,

"To Mrs. Wizzlepan, Upton Fields, Shropshire.   "DANIEL BOOKER."

"At all events," said Booker with a sigh, as he sealed the foregoing note, "I shall have some of my own kith and kin near me—that's one comfort; and perhaps it will be my only comfort, for I can't say that I feel the happiest person in the world. Heigh ho! why did I marry? Oh, why did I marry? why, I say?" and Mr. Booker looked around him, as if he expected some responding echo to afford him a substantial answer to the question. But as none did, he satisfied himself by making a pretence of pulling some of the hair out of his head; and then, as he found that Mrs. Booker was coming into the room, he put on an appearance of as much happiness as he could.

"My dear," he said, "I have written to my orphan niece, Amelia, to come here.'

"Certainly, my love; certainly. Anything you like, I'm sure I shall like; and any one who is pleasing company to you shall be pleasing company to me."

"That's very kind of you, my dear—very kind, indeed. Ahem! What an odd mad fellow that was who came to the house last night, and then made such a disturbance."

"Very odd, indeed; but in life we must expect to meet with odd characters; and, keeping a tavern, of course one is more liable to that sort of thing than in any other line of life. But it's not worth thinking of, after all."

"No, no. And yet I suppose foolish people really suppose now that there is a haunted room in this house?"

"Certainly they do. For my own part, I have no doubt that the party who made the disturbance last night had an ugly dream there."

"Oh, no doubt—no doubt. But what is said concerning that room? and why is it left so deserted, and yet furnished?"

"Why, they do say that it is haunted by some spirit who will let no one rest there; but I much wish you would really be so kind as to put an end to the idle superstition, by making it your bedroom for a week or so."

"With you, my dear?"

"Oh no! It is not for women to dare such adventures. You can go yourself, you know. Indeed it is the most comfortable room in the house—the quietest, airiest, warmest; and, as for an invalid's room, it is admirably adapted for such a purpose; and, I assure you——"

"Oh, you know that by experience, I suppose?"

"Well, I suppose I may say I do."

"What do you mean, my love, by saying, you suppose you may say you do?"

"I meant that I had not been ill there exactly myself, that was all; but as I have no secrets with you, my dear, I make no hesitation in telling you there have been some deaths in the room."

"Oh! The—the—the six husbands?"

"Yes, my love. But let us talk of a livelier theme than that. How struck I am with your generosity in effecting a life assurance in my favour."

"You are very welcome, my duck. I think I'll go and take a walk, and call upon my old friend Thompson."

"Do, my love, it will do you good, I assure you; and take care of yourself, and mind your come home now to lunch. Remember what an interest I have in you now, my dear, and, for my sake, take care of the crossings."

"D—n the crossings!" muttered Booker. "I shouldn't mind being run over at the first one I come to."

There were no railroads in those days, and the fast coaches were not over fast modes of travelling; so that some days elapsed before a hairy trunk, a bonnet box, a great basket, and a young lady of about seventeen, who rushed into Mr. Booker's arms, arrived at the Wheatsheaf, at Pimlico.

"Oh, Amelia, my dear," said Mr. Booker. "Is that you?"

"Yes, uncle; oh, yes."

"Why, how you have grown. Goodness gracious, when I last saw you, you were one——"

"I was twelve, uncle."

"I mean one of the children of the village, and now you are——"

"Seventeen, uncle."

"Upon my life! and good looking to."

"Yes, uncle."

"Yes, do you say—why, who told you so? You seem to be quite aware of the fact at all events."

"Dick Atterbury, uncle; I wouldn't have him; so he went and listed for a soldier, uncle, and I don't know what became of him at all. I dare say the French have *shooted* him dead, and I'm very sorry now—oh, I am—I am—I am! oh, dear! I am—I am! oh, oh, oh! I—I—oh, oh!"

"I shall be stunned," cried Mr. Booker. "My dear, do you think you can endure this sort

No. 3.

of thing, eh? She is not the sort of person exactly that I expected she would be. What do you think of her, my dear?"

"Oh, we shall soon rub off the country rust," said Mrs. Booker; "I dare say she is amiable enough; at all events, she has candour, we see, and if she be but simple, that is not the worst of qualities; moreover, she is your orphan niece, and that is sufficient for me."

"Upon my word, after all, she's an amiable woman," thought Booker.

"I'm much obliged to you, ma'am," said Amelia, "and if I am any trouble or too stupid, you can send me back again."

"You can't be too stupid," said Mrs. Booker. "Come along with me."

That evening Mr. Booker took his niece a walk in the park to show her some of the lions of the metropolis, and the more he talked to her, the more stupid he found her, and yet she was a buxom good-looking girl enough for all that, though rather weak in the upper story.

"My dear," he said, "that's the king's palace, there, you see, the palace of St. James, and that's called the garden-gate, where you see the sentinels reposing on their guns."

There came a shrill scream from Amelia, which so discomposed a dandified fellow who was aping her from the principal mall, that he fell down at once; but Amelia, heeding nothing, rushed up to one of the guards on duty at the garden-gate of the palace, and laying hold of him, exclaimed—

"Oh, Dick, it's you, it's you—I know it's you a guarding of the king's *palias*. It's you, Dick! Don't you know me? I'm Amelia."

"Know you, my angel? of course I do," said Dick; "but don't you see I'm on guard? For God's sake go away."

"Yes, yes, he knows me. Oh—oh—oh! It's Dick, and he's made a general or a corporal, I'll be bound; it's much the same, ain't it, which? Oh, dear! oh, dear! it's really Dick Atterbury."

It don't at any time take much trouble to collect a crowd in London, either in the park or elsewhere, and when the people began to collect, the soldier turned to Mr. Booker, saying—

"If you will tell me, sir, where to call upon her, I will do so as soon as I am relieved from duty; but if she goes on in this way, and makes a crowd collect round my post, it will the ruin of me."

Mr. Booker was a kind-hearted man enough, and he accordingly replied, as he dragged Amelia away by main force—

"You will find her, my good fellow, at the Wheatsheaf at Pimlico."

"Thank you, sir—thank you."

"And so it's really you, Dick, turned soldier. Oh, dear! oh, dear!"

"My dear, come away," said Mr. Booker; "for God's sake, come away! I can assure you that if the king were to come out and see you talking to Dick, the consequences might be very serious to him; so come away at once, and do not say any more about him. Don't you hear him say he will come and see you, so you can very easily spare him now. Come along, and don't cry, that's a good girl."

These remonstrances had the desired effect, and as the whole affair had not occupied many minutes, Mr. Booker got his niece away before the rapidly-assembling people knew very well what it was all about, and completely without compromising Dick in any way.

"My dear," said Mr. Booker, "you must really learn to control your feelings a little now you have come to London."

"Oh, but I can't."

"Oh, but you must. What would people think of you? Why, I verily believe that if I had not, at the moment I did, dragged you away, you would have thought nothing of throwing your arms about that soldier's neck."

"Oh, that I would."

"You would?"

"Oh, yes, uncle; you can't think how unhappy I have been ever since he went away, for you see I didn't mean him to go; but somehow he took me at my word. I was half a mind to go in disguise as a drummer boy myself."

"You—you?"

"Yes; I could have put on a pair of what-do-you-call-'ems, you know, uncle."

"Deuce take the girl," muttered Mr. Booker to himself. "She will be getting into a thousand scrapes in London. I wish to God she had remained in Shropshire. This comes of being too kind and generous; upon my word, those qualities won't do in this world."

Mr. Booker quite forgot that he had sent for his niece as much to keep him company as for any other reason, although he set the whole affair down to the score of his very great benevolence.

CHAPTER VII.

HOW SHERIDAN GOT BANTERED DREADFULLY, BUT WOULD NOT SEE THE JOKE.

"Hurrah, hurrah, bravo! Give him another cheer. Upon my word, Sherry, you improve, indeed you do. That was as good a one as you have told for a long time."

These words were spoken by Colonel Hill to Sheridan, after a supper in which the same parties we introduced in the first chapter of this work were engaged.

"As good a what?" said Sheridan

"Oh, oh, oh!"

"Well, gentlemen, you may say what you please, and think what you please; but nothing will divert my mind from the idea that I did see the ghost of Mrs. Widow Mortimer's husbands."

"You don't really mean to persevere in such a statement?"

"Indeed I do, though. Seeing is believing."

"Not always," said one who had not before spoken, "not always; I believe it is considered by many persons to be the greatest height of philosophy to doubt everything you see, and believe everything that you cannot understand."

"Well, well, as you please, gentlemen," said Sheridan; "you may be as sceptical as you like, I don't ask you to believe, I only asked you to listen while I told you something curious, and I trust you will fully admit that I have kept my word."

"Oh, you have certainly done that, but come now, Sherry," said he who was called George, "what conclusion do you draw from all this?"

"The conclusion I draw is in favour of the ghosts, and consequently against Mrs. Mortimer."

"Mrs. Booker, you mean; but you surely don't mean to assert that you believe the accusations?"

"No, I assert nothing—pray understand me. I admit all you have said from first to last about the possibility, nay, the probability, of its being, after all, nothing but a dream. It is true, I sat down by a fire at an hour of the night when one may be supposed at all events ready for sleep, although we seldom think of that necessary mode of recruiting the human frame until long after midnight. I was alone—and when that is the case, I often feel a somnolescent influence stealing over me; so I fairly admit it may have been a dream."

"May have been, indeed," said George; "of course it was. Now I'll tell you what happened to me once, and you may fancy what an effect it was likely to have upon me, if I had not felt quite sure it was nothing but a dream."

"Hear, hear, hear."

"Well, gentlemen, you know that about this time last year, I and a certain illustrious personage did not quite agree about a variety of matters, and we had rather a serious interview; so serious, indeed, that when I left St. James's, the illustrious personage happened to say that he hoped the threshold of that great regal building would not be again polluted by my footsteps until I came to my senses, or something to that effect."

"I recollect," said Sherry.

"Well, as you may all be well aware, I was sufficiently nettled at this, and made up my mind that it should be some time before my foot crossed the threshold of St. James's, and I had a bedroom prepared for me in the speaker's house, at Westminster—the old house, you know."

"Yes, yes—go on."

"It was one of the best rooms in the place—large and lofty, with deep-set windows, and a carved marble chimney-piece of most extraordinary beauty. A large bedstead was in it, a carpet had been hastily laid down, and the place made as comfortable as it could in a few hours' notice; and, rather out of spirits, I must confess, and——"

"In spirits likewise," said Sherry, imitating some one drinking.

"No, no—upon honour, no. My affairs were gloomy, positively gloomy: I was as sober as a judge."

"Which of them?"

"Now this is too bad, Sherry; I let you tell your story, and why cannot you be equally indulgent towards me?"

"A thousand pardons; I won't say another word."

"Very good. Well, I went to this room that had been prepared for me, as I have mentioned, about a quarter to twelve o'clock; and I sincerely meant to go to sleep if I could, and not to lie awake, thinking over disagreeables, as sometimes I had done. There was a good bright fire blazing on the hearth; I declined all attendance, and was soon between the sheets. The palace clock struck twelve—I could hear it quite plainly, and then just as it came to the last stroke, the clock of St. Margaret's, by the Abbey, struck twelve likewise; but I was not thinking of anything approaching to the supernatural, and it seemed to me that I lay and watched the fire go gradually down until there was nothing of it left but a few dull red embers at the bottom of the grate.

" And then you went to sleep."

" Perhaps I did ;—nay, I think I did; at all events, I was in that state between sleeping and waking, when the imagination is far more master of the brain than the judgment."

" Well, well."

" Blame yourself for the interruption. Suddenly there was a strange white sort of a light in the room, and at first I thought it must be the beams of the moon that had darted into the room, either in consequence of that luminary rounding some obstacle, or——"

" Hold !" said Sheridan, " the moon is not a luminary."

" Well, well—never mind—there was a white light in the room which made every object faintly visible, as if seen through one of those white mists which on a summer's morning hang over a landscape. I looked up, and for the first time a sensation of great fear came over me, for I saw that I was not alone.

" In the centre of the room, which was some eight or ten feet from the foot of the bed, I saw some shadowy-looking forms, who, from their gestures, appeared to be conversing. I listened to them, and after a time I made out what one of them was saying.

" 'Harry,' he said, in a solemn tone, ' it is many a day since one who will wear England's crown lay down to repose in this apartment. He will wear it, but not happily. You have filled the old hall of Westminster with throngs to witness a royal trial, and so will he.'

" 'He will,' said another ; ' but the Sybarite will live long. Shall we speak now to him of that which is to come ?'

" ' No, no, no,' said several.

" My curiosity was strangely excited, and I started up in bed, saying—

" ' Stay, stay ! and if you can read to me the book of the future, do so. I will not shrink.'

" The forms gradually wasted away, and, as I saw the face of one, I never was so much struck as by its amazing likeness to the eighth Henry's portrait, which is in the east gallery at St. James's. In another minute, I suppose, owing to hearing me call, some one who was keeping watch in the outer room came in, and said—

" ' Did your highness call ?'

" ' No,' I replied; ' but are you sure no one has been into the room ?'

" ' Quite sure, your highness. The back of the chair in which I sat was against the door of the apartment, your highness, and there is no other entrance.'

" ' Very well. Good night.'

" ' I have the honour of wishing your highness profound repose.'

" And so I was alone again. What do you think of that now?"

" It's easily enough explained," said Sheridan ; " you were sleeping in a chamber that had been at one time, no doubt, occupied by the eighth Henry, and that was his ghost."

" Ah, you are now on the task of defending supernatural appearances, Sherry, in order to keep yourself in due countenance about your own ghosts at the Wheatsheaf."

" As you please, as you please."

" Well, but," said Colonel Hill, " you don't mean, Sherry, to do anything in the matter."

" No, not absolutely, although I would—

'Take the ghost's words for a thousand pounds.'

But I shall not lose sight of the Wheatsheaf and its occupants, I assure you; and if there be anything that goes far towards a verification of what the ghosts have asserted, I shall feel that something ought to be done."

" Agreed, agreed ; but for Heaven's sake, Sherry, do not expose yourself to the ridicule of taking steps in any matter consequent upon supernatural circumstances."

" Rest assured I will not. But I will tell you of a comical thing that happened in the park to-day. You must know poor Booker—I call him poor Booker, because I think he he is booked —has got his niece home from Shropshire, a young and pretty girl enough, and she found a former lover of hers, who had enlisted on account of her cruelty, mounting guard at the garden-gate of St. James's. Booker had enough to do to get her away, you must know, for the girl was so overjoyed at seeing him, that she nearly took the post by storm."

" Capital, capital."

" It would have been the finest fun in the world if an illustrious personage had happened to to see it."

" Male or female illustrious?" said Hill.

"Oh, both, both, to be sure. But look how serious George looks. He is thinking of Booker's niece."

"No, I am not; but don't carry your royal allusions beyond the heir apparent. Do you understand?"

"Quite; there was no harm meant. *Honi soit qui mal y pense.* But the niece of this Booker is pretty, and a most horrible simpleton; a thorough country wench as regards health and stamina, and yet without vulgarity. There might be some rare fun, if one could get her here for a few moments, and persuade her to meet the soldier somewhere."

"And why not—why not?"

"Well, I don't mind, I'm ready and willing; but whose game is she to be?"

"Mine," said George, "mine to be sure, whose else? I run all the risks. If anybody suffers afterwards, is it not I? This game is mine."

"No, no, that's not fair. Let the girl herself decide; we will all assist in the affair and give each an equal chance. The first man that she uses an endearing epithet to, let him be the conqueror."

"An endearing epithet! what endearing epithet?"

"If she says, 'I love you,' to any one of us, that ought to be sufficient; and now, gentlemen, you can set your wits to work to see how the fond confession is to be coaxed or bullied out of the girl, and we must arrange some plan to get her to some place where the trial can be made."

"What say you to the gardens of Buckingham House?" said George. "It's near at hand, and I have a pass-key to all its entrances."

"Good, good."

"Then shall we consider that as quite settled?"

"Of course. But I don't approve of having the soldier too much in the way, mind you. He is rather a determined-looking young fellow, and might be positively troublesome."

"Oh, if he were, we could soon put him out of harm's way, by getting him into the hands of the guard; and, besides, when he finds his mistress false, he will probably console himself, as most of his class do, by a drop of something strong."

"Then, Sherry, you are to be the conductor of the adventure. I will meet the girl in the gardens, if you will contrive to bring her there; and I can only say that I shall, of course, be very much obliged."

"Perhaps," thought Sherry, "you will not be so profuse of your acknowledgments by the time the adventure is quite over, Master George. We shall see."

CHAPTER VIII.

SHOWS HOW AMELIA WAS DECOYED INTO THE GARDENS OF BUCKINGHAM HOUSE.

THE prince was not quite a match for Sheridan in intrigue, but yet he fancied he was, and, for a time, he was most certainly under an impression that Sheridan would take the trouble of decoying Amelia Booker to the gardens of Buckingham House, in order that he then might try how fascinating he could be to the country girl.

But Sheridan had his own views in the matter, and he thought that the opportunity of carrying them out, in the private gardens of Buckingham House, was not to be despised.

"Ah, Maria," he said, as he strutted into the Wheatsheaf, "what shall I say to you for all the trouble I gave you when I slept, or pretended to sleep, in the haunted room?"

"Oh, don't think of it, sir," said Maria, who, what with one and another, was very well paid—"don't think of it, sir; I am only sorry you should have had such a bad dream, though. Did you really see a ghost, sir?"

"Not a ghost, Maria, but a legion of ghosts. However, that's not the question just at present. I believe you have an addition to the household, have you not?"

"Oh, yes, we have Mr. Booker's niece, Miss Amelia, from Shropshire; but between you and me, sir, and the post, she's no more idea of—God bless me, there's Mrs. Booker's bell, sir—than you have. What was I saying? There's the bell again. Dear me, what a trouble to be sure it is!"

"I must have a few more particulars from this girl," thought Sherry, "at all events;" and when Maria came back, he said—

"Are you aware that Amelia has a kind of sweetheart—a soldier in the Guards?"

"Oh dear yes, we have heard all about that; and the fact is, he is expected to call here,

Only think, a soldier, sir—a common soldier! Well, I wouldn't stoop and pick up nothing. A common soldier—pah! I'm surprised. But here she comes: for my sake, sir, don't say I said anything about it."

Amelia came into the bar-parlour at this moment, and finding some one there, was about to leave; but Sheridan rose and made so polite a bow, that she was compelled to return it with a bobbing country curtsey, as if she were actually going to sit down on the floor.

"Don't go, miss, on my account," said Sherry, as Maria left them alone a moment to attend to a customer. "The fact is, I have got something to say to you."

"To me, sir?" Oh, gemini!"

"Oh, what?"

"Nothing, sir: I only wondered what a fine gentleman like you could have to say to me."

"It's just this, Amelia:—Your lover, the soldier, wants to meet you alone this evening, at dusk, by the walling of the gardens of Buckingham House, close at hand, and he charges me to tell you not to tell anybody about it, for he has something to say to you of a very secret character indeed, so you must say nothing to anybody."

"Well, but—oh, gracious—oh—oh—oh!"

"Why, what's the matter—what's the matter?"

In another moment a smart looking young fellow of a soldier made his way into the bar-parlour, and was about to clasp Amelia in his arms, when Sheridan rose suddenly, and with a face bearing the most portentous aspect, said—

"Hush! for Heaven's sake, hush! You are the—the—yes, the lover of the—the—the niece of Mr. Booker. Thank God I am in here! Young man, come this way, and I will tell you something that will astonish you, and, above all things, you must not be seen here—mind that."

"Well, I was——"

"I knew it. Come along. Hush!"

"Well, but," said Amelia——"

"You are quite right—this way, young sir: you shall have the most substantial reasons, and if you truly love——"

"But, sir——"

"Very true—not another word—come along—come along—all's right—all's right—that will do: and now that we are outside the house I can unbosom my mind to you. You know Brummel?"

"What! he whom they call Beau Brummel, the acquaintance of the prince? Oh, yes, certainly I do, by sight."

"Well, what I wanted to tell you was this—that Brummel, you understand, has taken a violent fancy to Amelia, that he has induced Mrs. Mortimer to assist him, and, at this very moment, is with her. Hush! now don't be violent. He will meet Amelia to-night, at eight, in the park, close to the entrance of Birdcage-walk, and what you ought to do is, to leave Amelia to make the appointment, and to keep it if she likes, and then pounce upon them both, upbraid her, and punish the libertine. This will be poetical justice."

"At Birdcage-walk? Curse him!"

"You may well say that. And she to listen to him."

"Yes: she has listened to him, but she is not lost. If you like, of course you can go back to the Wheatsheaf, and there Mrs. Mortimer will see you, and the plan of assignation will be altered, that's all, so that neither you nor I will know where it is. That was why I have pulled you out as I have."

"Thank you, thank you. Confound his impertinence! I'll—I'll—but no matter—no matter. Perhaps, sir, whoever you are, you will hear something of this matter to morrow. I loved the girl—nay, it is useless paltering with my own feelings—I love her still; and if I can help it, she shall not fal a victim to that puppy—that tailor's show board—that stilted piece of buckram —d—n him!"

"You are quite right, very right; and the feelings you express upon this occasion are just what any one would expect from you. What will you do?"

"Do—do? Why, then, of course, what else should I do? and I will give the jackanapes a dressing that will, perhaps be of a different description to any he has had yet. At eight o'clock you say, sir? Eight o'clock, at the park end of Birdcage-walk?"

"Precisely. I have told you this, because I really have a natural abhorrence to see innocence destroyed. Of course, all that he wants is, to have an intrigue to boast of to the prince and his dissolute companions, and I must confess I should like you to baulk him."

"I will, you may depend, sir. You may depend I will, and with many thanks to you for the information you have given me upon the subject, sir, I bid you good day, and if ever it lies in my power to do you a good turn, I can only say that I shall be very happy to do so."

"Oh, don't mention it, I have only done as I would wish, and fully expect to be done by."

When Sherry made sure that the soldier believed the whole affair, and had no intention of spoiling the plot by going back to the Wheatsheaf, he at once betook himself to Half Moon-street, Piccadilly, where, in a certain first floor, in' a certain house, resided a lady who, from being a great favourite of Master George, had become as great an aversion; and as Sherry knew that the lady would eagerly take part in any adventure which promised a return of her influence, he had no doubt of succeeding in what he was about.

"My dear madam," he said, "you know I have always acted a friendly part towards you."

"I am well aware of that," said the lady. "Is there any hope?"

"I know to what you allude, and as to whether there be any hope or not of a return of a certain person's affections, I know not; but you have written to me several times to know if I would exert myself to get you an interview."

"And to which you returned me no answer."

"Yes, but that was neither neglect, my dear madam, nor disinclination. The fact was, I always kept on delaying my answer until I should have something to say, and now you see that I have, and am come personally to assure you of my good offices and my regard."

The lady affected to be satisfied, whether she was or not; but, when Sheridan continued what he had to say, her real gratification was apparent.

"You must know," he said, "that, although I did not write to you so much, I was constantly pestering you know who, to grant you an audience, which he always refused; but I had so set my heart upon getting one for you, that now I am actually going, and am fearful to commit myself very much by so doing. You shall see him this evening if you like."

"If I like! Can you doubt it?"

"Not at all. But you will quite understand that I throw myself upon your honour in the affair, for my position would be an awkward one if it were known that I had encouraged this matter for you."

"Oh, rely upon me. Let what will happen, I shall not mention you."

"Very good, I am quite satisfied. I will tell you, then, that he is going to have a meeting to-night, by the little garden-gate of Buckingham House, with one who, if she once get the mastery of him, will retain it to the utter exclusion of you or anybody else for ever."

Fire flashed from the lady's eyes at the idea of a rival, but she was silent through intense anxiety to know all that Sherry had to tell her; and he added—

"Yes, a rival! He will meet her at dusk by the wall of the garden; now, what is to hinder you from taking her place, if I keep her back a little—your own tact must do the rest; I can only give you the opportunity, you know; you can but fail and have a scene with him—and if you do, you are not worse off than now."

"Certainly not; I have no objection in the world, and am mightily obliged to you into the bargain; I will wrap myself up in my cardinal, and then he will not know me until I please. I suppose it's a—a young person?"

"Yes and very nearly as handsome as yourself."

"The wretch!"

"Well, well, we will consider that as all settled then; you meet me at the garden gate a little before dusk, and I will tell you if all is right, and when the prince speaks to you, mind you be coy and irresolute; but let him persuade you into the garden as soon as possible, and if you say anything speak in a feigned voice, and say, ' Oh, if the soldier should come, what would he say?' "

"I will obey your instructions to the very letter."

Sheridan requested, as he was there, that she would favour him with the loan of a pen and a sheet of paper, as he wished to write a note, and when she complied with his desire, he in a most lady-like hand wrote as follows—

"To Mr. Brummel.

"Sir.—To see you is to—ah! excuse me that I cannot write the word, love! but if you will be at the Birdcage-walk to-night at eight, you will meet one who at length yields to your many solicitations for a private meeting."

This note he sealed with a seal which the lady lent to him, and when he left her lodgings, he gave a boy sixpence to take it to Mr. Brummel's house in Bolton-street, where the dandy kept a very *recherche* establishment, that was the wonder of the town, inasmuch as nobody knew where the money came from.

Sheridan laughed to himself as he said—

"Well, I think I have managed all that very well; Beau Brummel will go to the assignation and meet the enraged soldier; George will decoy an old pigeon into the gardens of the palace, and I shall have freedom of speech with the fair Amelia; and yet why should I miss the fun at Buckingham House? I will not either—certainly not; I will tell George that I have a fair one whom I wish to meet, and get him to do me the favour of leaving the garden gate open for me. That will be rare sport—well, well, they may laugh at me about the ghosts of the Widow Mortimer's six husbands; but when they begin that, I shall turn the conversation towards the transactions of to-night."

Acting upon this resolution, this wild, reckless son of jollity sought the prince and easily obtained the permission he sought, regarding the use of the gardens of Buckingham House. Morality was rather low just then, and it was not much thought of by either party; we shall soon see what becomes of it, and we imagine that the coming night will be an amusing, if not an eventful one.

CHAPTER IX.

DETAILS HOW MRS. MORTIMER WAS A LITTLE GIVEN TO SUPERSTITION, AND PAID DEARLY FOR IT.

"I CANNOT think where Mrs. B— has gone," said Mr. Booker, as he sat smoking in the bar-parlour, on the same evening that the experiment upon the constancy of Amelia to her military lover was to be made in the gardens of Buckingham House. "She went out, I believe, Maria?"

"Yes, she did," replied Maria, after a pause of some moments; and she continued to arrange some glasses that had been displaced some short time previously.

"Have you any idea as to where she could have gone?" said Mr. Booker, who was engaged in smoking and thinking by turns. "Didn't she say anything?"

"Nothing," replied Maria, without stopping in her employment—"nothing at all; but she had dressed herself, and had on one of her best gowns, so that she has gone somewhere where she wishes to be seen well-dressed. She went, I believe, towards Westminster."

"Towards Westminster!" said Mr. Booker. "Who has she gone to there? She did not tell me a word about it. It's very singular, but I suppose I shall understand it all, when it's made plain," muttered Mr. Booker to himself.

"Perhaps she has only gone for a walk," remarked Maria.

"Perhaps so," said Mr. Booker; but he was hardly conscious of having spoken, for his thoughts were otherwise occupied at that moment.

In the meanwhile Mrs. Booker walked towards Westminster by herself, as if no one had the remotest interest in her proceedings. To be sure, now and then she turned round to look behind her, and then ascertained that she was alone, and no curious and prying eyes were fixed upon her, and that nothing but a purely accidental encounter could reveal her locality to any one.

It does happen that accidents often reveal the petty weaknesses of individuals, and which little salient points they are always most anxious to hide and conceal from general observation; and therefore, to prevent any such occurrence, she dropped her veil over her face, which she thought would preclude all possibility of recognition.

Thus safe, she turned, and went boldly forward, until she came to a very quiet and retired street, at the corner of which she paused and looked round.

It is singular that those matters in which women place, perhaps, more faith than anything else, they are the more anxious to hide from men in particular, and usually from each other. Their belief in superstitious observances and the powers of fore-knowledge is, even at this day, almost universal.

This is no untruth nor exaggeration, and will be found to be correct, if all that which is known to the individual were known to many; if the little secret acts and thoughts were to be permitted to see the daylight, then the world would know more than is deemed now at all likely, or probable—nay, possible.

After having gazed a few moments up and then down the street wistfully enough, she walked briskly down the street.

After she had got about half-way down the street, she paused before a dirty, dingy-looking house, in which appeared no signs of, at best, a respectable habitation, though it was large and roomy enough.

She walked hastily up the steps, pushed the door in a peculiar manner, and then walked in as the door opened before her.

The door opening showed a bare passage, through which she walked, and when the door was closed behind her, she secured it, and then paused a while. A little bell handle hung on the right hand, and a wire ran therefrom to an old wire above, that led away upstairs. It was an odd-looking piece of ivory, much in the shape of the haft of a knife, but there it was, carved and suspended to the wire.

Mrs. Booker took hold of this implement, and pulling it, a small tinkling, silvery sound was heard from up stairs.

At the foot of the stairs was a small gate, which opened of itself, and when Mrs. Booker saw this, she walked on, evidently understanding that she was to do so, and considered the opening of the gate as the signal for admission.

She walked up stairs, and when she got on the first floor, she was met by a large door

which prevented her from rising any higher, but in a moment more that opened, and a voice was heard to say—

"Welcome hither."

She walked up another flight of stairs, but yet this was not done without something like a deal of panting, and want of breath, for she had walked up so quickly. But, when she came to the landing again, she saw a door open before her, through which she passed, and entered a small room that was but partially lighted, where she paused.

Here were various hieroglyphics and matters that were hung about, of a confused and extraordinary character, and where there was space, there were strange characters and stuffed animals

No 4.

but she did not remain here long, for a small door suddenly swung open, and displayed to her view another room, and a voice was heard, saying—

"Come in—wait not, but come in."

She at once entered the room, and took a chair which appeared to be inviting her, and fixed her eyes upon a man, whose long beard and bushy eyelids were remarkable.

His figure was striking as he sat; he appeared tall and bulky, covered from head to foot in a frock of black velvet, confined at the neck and waist by bands, in which were wrought figures of beasts and reptiles in silver, surmounted by a high cap of sable, from which depended some cords of silver lace.

He sat in an arm-chair; before him was a table, on which was spread many extraordinary matters and some loose books, one of which was open.

"The old question?" said the conjurer.

Mrs. Booker did not reply for a moment, but took counsel for herself, and felt indisposed to admit the truth of the implied inquiry, even to a conjurer; but she thought that as she knew so much, she had better blink the question, and not deny it, as she had upon the first impulse intended to do, and turn it off in some other channel.

"Speak!" said the conjurer.

"A little information," replied Mrs. Booker, leisurely,—"only a little information. You have seen me before. I believe you remember me?"

"I never forget," said the conjurer, "I never forget! What once enters the portals of the mind is never forgotten by me."

Mrs. Booker paused upon this, considered, and then said—

"I would wish to know whether I am to be lucky, or not; fortunate, or otherwise?"

"Why," said the conjurer, looking at some ciphers in the book; and then taking a pen, he cast up some figures, and turning to an instrument not unlike a telescope, but shorter and bigger, he applied his eye to one end of it, and turned it round and round in its stand, which consisted of two rings of brass, supported upon two cross rods, set in marble,—"why, as to that question, I see that the stars of the past have been bright and clear—you have been fortunate, and there is no positive intelligence to the contrary."

"Are there any possibilities?"

"Yes, there is one, which may be overcome, however, if you take the proper means, which, as I read the stars, you will, and all will be well again; but you will make a closer acquaintance with one whom you have known but slightly."

Mrs. Booker mentally considered what all this could mean, and she began to cast about in her own mind those of her acquaintance whom she knew little of, and who were not on very intimate terms, but, at the same time, whom she thought were likely to become useful or entertaining in any way whatever; but she could not think of any one whom she could hit upon as at all likely.

"You are thinking," said the conjurer, "in your mind, whom you are likely to make another acquaintance with. You may save yourself the trouble, for that you cannot now do; you will find all this out in time."

"I dare say," said Mrs. Booker, "but have you really nothing else to say?"

"It does not become one of my profession to say much; great as may be my knowledge, yet it is not for every ear to hear it. There are a few whose education and whose knowledge of the world may fit them to receive such truths as the lights of science may shed."

"Do you possess these lights?" inquired Mrs. Booker.

"I do," replied the seer,—"I do, or else I am wasting my time in vain—quite in vain."

"Can you tell me anything that I only know, which no one knows but myself? Tell me that, and then I can give credit for what you say."

"Nay, I have told you so much already that you must know that no one else could at all foretel, and which you could not have known. Confess it; you know my skill, and can attest to the truth of my predictions and my assertions."

"Certainly," said Mrs. Booker, "certainly; I have no occasion to speak ill of you. You are a most extraordinary man—a very extraordinary man."

"That is admission enough."

"Then proceed to tell me of those things I most desire to hear."

"You shall be fortunate, if you choose that path that leads to fortune, or that which enables you to retain the good you have."

"I am willing to do that," replied Mrs. Booker; "yet what I am to do must be pointed out, if I am to follow any line that does not yet appear, until it does, or I cannot aid by the information you have given me."

"When the occasion comes, the course to be pursued will force itself upon you; you cannot mistake. The heavenly spheres do not point out more minutely what should be done. It cannot be expected that they should do more than point out, in a general manner, the course of human events."

" I thought each soul had its particular star ?"

" And so it has."

" And that it spoke plainly the events of life ?"

" And so it does," replied the seer. " It is written that you should see many, and yet none should be your lord long."

" Oh, does it say so much ?"

" Yes. When the event is extraordinarily great and important, then, indeed, there are combinations that point out that event ; but, should it be unimportant, then it is but generally described, which is as much as things are noted. It would take too much time to read the book of fate so minutely ; and, instead of finding out the occurrences that relate to man, generally, it would be a loss of time spent in the pursuit of one."

This was so evident, that Mrs. Booker had nothing to gainsay it or to object to it. That being the case, she paused a while to gain breath, and said—

" How can you study the stars in this place, and at all hours of the day ?"

" I have the means. I can show you the combinations which they form, producing all that is beautiful, in colour and form."

" Can you, indeed ?" said Mrs. Booker. " I should like to see such very much indeed."

" You shall for once be gratified—at all events, for once," said the conjurer, drawing to him the instrument through which he had been looking.

" By looking into this," he continued, " you may see all the colours that are to be found in the rainbow. You will find them all amalgamate, and then split asunder in all the variety of shapes that can be imagined ; these combinations are rare and beautiful. You may look in at this end, and then tell me what you see."

Mrs. Booker did look into the instrument. There was a beautiful combination of colours, and then she observed there was a slow motion in it, which caused the combination to dissolve gradually, and to vanish ; but in the place of the old there was a new one."

These changes went on for some minutes, until, being tired, Mrs. Booker withdrew her eye, and the conjuror then said—

" What think you of my instrument ?"

" Beautiful ! I never saw anything so extraordinary before."

" No," said the sage, proudly. " None could exhibit such, save those who have spent their boyhood and manhood in hard and severe thought, and then they must be blessed by good fortune and teachers, else they never thrive."

" But of what use can that beautiful thing be for your purposes ?"

" That can only be learned by long and tedious study ; but I, who have endured all this, can read in every combination a different sentence—sometimes a volume—which tells me what I want so much to know. The art of telling what those combinations mean, is the *sine qua non* of astrology—without it you can do nothing."

" It is strange," muttered Mrs. Booker—"very strange."

" So it is ; but, more than that, you must approach them with an honesty of purpose—nay, those who come to read their destinies, if they come with a lie in their mouth, the information they gain will not assist them—it will be a mere mockery."

" Well," said Mrs. Booker, " I have said nothing but what is true, and am quite content that all my labour shall become nothing, if I have said anything in the way of deceit, for I have told you nothing ; therefore, I have nothing to be charged with."

" Exactly ; and now say what more you desire ?"

" Shall I again become a widow, or do the stars promise me a longer reign of happiness than will permit me to again wear those sad and mournful weeds ? Tell me that, for it most interests me to know."

The seer gazed through his instrument again, and then turned to his book, which he consulted with some care, and having found some results, noted them down in a book ; he made some calculations, which he transferred upon paper, and then he paused some moments, as if deliberating in his own mind, and said—

" Yes, the fates will that you lose a husband once again—the stars look gloomy, and Saturn reigns supreme."

" It will be unfortunate," said the lady, with a sigh.

" Yes, it will be unfortunate," replied the seer, " very unfortunate, indeed, to you ; but it is to be hoped, indeed, 'tis written, that you will not injure your health by fretting ; it may be, that you will have cause to rejoice in the change."

"I cannot conceive such a thing."

"Perhaps not, but such things have happened ere now, you know."

"Oh, yes, yes," said Mrs. Booker. I am not disputing the possibility, I only have not yet had any cause to dread such a thing—and I hope I never may."

"The decrees of fate admit of no dispute, and when once known, there is no hope. Fate and Hope are directly opposed to each other, and when the one approaches the other flies."

"When will such an event most likely take place?" inquired Mrs. Booker. "It behoves me to know so much, for the evil, if far off, will give me time to hope it may not be here, and spend some happy hours ere the destroyer steal his victim."

"The ides of March will not give place to the warmer days of April ere you again become a widow, and once again wear those weeds you have so lately doffed; the hand of Fate points out the event from which there's no escape."

CHAPTER X.

THE UNEXPECTED ARRIVAL.—THE WIDOW IN A NEW CHARACTER.

THIS answer of the seer to Mrs. Booker appeared to give her great satisfaction, and she paused to consider, in her own mind, what next question she could frame to cover the last. In a short time, however, she said—

"Well, and am I again so soon to become sad and forlorn? Well, Providence knows best what is good for us, and hides from us its meaning; and that's why, I suppose, we are apt apparently to repine at its decrees, when we ought, in fact, to rejoice; and we should, no doubt, if we knew the end that it was to accomplish."

"Indeed, none can read the object, though we can see the way; and yet the stars look kindly on you. There is one black spot, but that is capable of removal."

"Does it denote danger?"

"Yes, but merely a threat—one that may be bought off, I imagine, by some means that circumstances will point out; to neglect which would be to encounter some dreadful alternative, which appears to me to involve some terrible extremity."

"Well," said Mrs. Booker, "you have said so much. Am I to get over it, am I to take the alternative, or am I to refuse it? But, if I am to be the conqueror over circumstances, which you say are portentous, and only to be overcome in one way, that way must be adopted."

"Just so."

"Then I am to accept of whatever lesser evil that may be presented for my notice?"

"Exactly so; but, at the same time, I do not see how you can consider an alternative in the way of a lesser evil. It may be an alternative, and yet not be such."

"Well, well, that may be so; I will not dispute, though it appears to me that it usually does take away hope sooner or later."

"I will not dispute points that are so nicely balanced as to require a cool discrimination to see the clear and great disparity."

"Well, well, that does not matter. I am the victor, or am to be so, that is all. I think I needn't trouble myself about it, save to feel regret at the sorrowful fortune in store for me. I am sad and regretful in the extreme. My sorrows will be enduring."

"There will be something that will turn your regret into joy, or something very much like it; so it is written, and I can but read the book as it is before me."

"Precisely," replied the widow; "'tis as I would wish to hear it, else false intelligence would be the result to me."

At that moment an attendant entered the room, and whispered something in the ear of the astrologer, who started and uttered the words—

"What, has he come—the marquis?"

"Yes, sir, he has come, and waits for you below, and says his business is important, and must see you immediately. I had much ado to keep him back at all. He was for following me up stairs, but I shut the door upon him on the stairs, and he cannot come up higher, though he won't go down again. What a noise he's making—he won't be quiet—he's quite impatient, and wants to see you, and wonders why he's kept."

As the attendant spoke, there came a loud knocking at the stairs door, and a voice called out something undistinguishable.

"Go down and keep him in talk for a few minutes, and delay time as long as you can; and when you can't help it, he must come up as he will."

The attendant departed, and the astrologer, who appeared annoyed, and at the same time in some little puzzle what to do, suddenly turned to Mrs. Booker, and after a moment's thought said to her—

"I have some gentleman come to see me, he's a marquis; and I expect it's only about some frivolous matter or other; but, nevertheless, I'll make you privy to all that is said or done. You will, of course, be silent and secret?"

"I will," replied Mrs. Booker, "so that there may be no discovery, as I am anxious that I shall not be seen here. I'll remain quiet, and what is said will be a secret in my breast, depend upon it. I'll never breathe a word about it."

"Should you do so, it will act adversely to your interest, I can assure you; but I will not deem you capable of any baseness. But no man or woman ever throve for them. I can evoke the spirits that wait at my beck, and can cause much evil."

"I will promise," said the widow—"I will promise that you shall find me faithful; if you have any further doubt I will pass out."

"No, no, open that door and walk in—shut the door quick. Here he comes—here he comes."

Mrs. Booker hastened to the door that was pointed out to her, and entered a large closet in which was placed an arm-chair. She waited but to see this, and then drew the door to, just as the marquis entered. He was announced by the attendant as the Marquis Marchmont, and then the door was closed by an attendant.

"Upon my word," said the marquis, half angrily, half gaily, who was a man of nearly the middle age, good-looking, but evidently a *roue*—"upon my word you keep people waiting below on the steps, in the passage, and on the stairs, as if you thought every man and woman were a thief-taker or peace-officer. What is the meaning of it?"

"I was busy, my lord, very busy."

"Calculating villany, I dare say."

"Why, my lord, you see so much of that is inherent in human nature, that in calculating human actions, I have to deal with many such matters as those your lordship speaks of."

"How tender you are not to name them aright."

"No, my lord, I have no regard for them; I merely look upon them as principles of human nature; and therefore, as such, the particular complexion it takes matters not to me."

"I see you are too philosophical to heed them in any shape; but, my fine wise man of the stars, your aid is in request."

"It is always at your lordship's commands, but now 'tis an evil hour with me. I would not engage in aught now, because I have one on hand, and while that is unfinished, it will scarcely be possible to enter successfully into any new matter."

"You want but to enhance your fee—psha!"

"No, my lord—no; it might be useless."

"It would; but I want you to speak upon matters that are not celestial—not at all connected with the spheres, but a plain matter of earth—nay, I will descend lower, a mere matter of paste-board and paint. Do you comprehend?"

The philosopher made a pantomimic motion with his hands, as a person does who shuffles and cuts playing cards.

"Excellent, excellent! I am quite satisfied with the greatness of your comprehension; you are a prince of conjurers—a very monarch! and now if you do not do cleverly what I require, I will not honour you with my acquaintance again."

"Your lordship is very good, but now is not the time."

"Now is the time, my prince of bell-metal—you ring true. Come, show me the trick—you knew it well; you know it, too, in an inimitable manner. Tell me the trick—show me the manner, and you know your reward."

"My lord, there is no trick a better sleight of hand; but I am almost palsied now, and cannot do what you require of me. 'Tis useless to ask more; I would at once consent, were it not as I say. My will is good—but some other time, my lord."

"No time like the time present, that beats all other times hollow; now don't you see——"

"My lord, hear me—I cannot do it now, I am too deeply immersed in other calculations, and it is a rule through which I cannot break—one which has never been broken by me."

"Then why did you see me?"

"Because your lordship would come up and force yourself in. Had it not been so, I should not have seen you, but still I cannot break this rule; my attendant endeavoured to tell you that I could not see you, and tried to prevent you."

"Yes, yes, I know that; but I did not believe that you really meant it to me, and you can easily explain what I require in a few minutes."

"I cannot now."

"Well, what am I to think of this? Really, Mr. Philosopher, or Mr. Conjurer, you might give me the required information that is wanted of you; you are as imperious as an Alexander, or a Cæsar. Come, come, be complaisant for once."

"No, no," said the philosopher, shaking his head; no, no."

"I am going out to-night, and I wanted to make a beginning. I should have been round to-morrow and related the success of the trick. Here are the cards, which are, as you will see, new. Now, come, let us see the trick. I have particular reasons; there's the Lady Fanny, who is a great hand at cards, and tries to drive me out of luck with her cards, and her eyes dazzle me, so that I sometimes lose there what I may gain elsewhere. I must, therefore, make up elsewhere by extra industry and luck; you see, I am in need of your aid."

"I see, my lord, and your lordship must see that I cannot do it. It is just what you asked me to do before, and I refused it."

"Well, since you won't be so accommodating as to do now what I wish you, when will you? I know it is impossible to make a bear smile with a tender cranium, but just be so accommodating as to do that. I thought you were a man of business; but, I suppose, you have some other business which you fancy more important; but you are in error."

"Very good, my lord, I will be at your service to-night or to-morrow."

"Very well; then, I will be here to-morrow. I shall be unable to come to-night; but be it so. I will be here at your time, since mine will not please you."

As the Marquis Marchmont spoke, he arose, and languidly lounged out of the place, and the conjurer rang a bell, which was answered by the attendant, who watched the Marquis out of the house, and when that was done, the conjurer arose and walked to the closet in which Mrs. Booker had entered.

But what was his amazement and consternation when he discovered that individual seated in the chair either asleep, or in a fit.

He coughed and hemmed; but no notice was taken of it, and then he spoke; but still no notice, and then he spoke again. He took her hand and shook her, and found that she had really fainted away, and was quite insensible.

Alarmed at this occurrence, he carried her out with some exertion, and bathing her temples with cold water, he forced a small quantity of some liquid down her throat, which had the effect of quickly restoring her sensation, for she sighed heavily, and opened her eyes, and gazed wildly about her, and then she exclaimed—

"Where is he? Where is he?"

"Whom do you mean?" inquired the conjurer.

"The marquis—the man who has been here."

"Gone. Do you know him?" inquired the conjurer. "'Tis the Marquis Marchmont—do you know him?"

"Speak not of him. I do not know him."

"But why all this emotion—something strange must have happened at one time or another?"

"I have known him, and know nothing of him that I would wish repeated again."

"But you appear to be much agitated."

"Cease to speak to me about him. I will tell you this much—I live but to seek vengeance upon that man; I will inflict such a vengeance upon him as shall serve as a mark—as an estimate of my injury—my hatred."

"How did all this arise?"

"Cease to ask any more now—let me go," she added, rising. "I will go now, another time I will relate to you more of this matter. I will tell you what it is that is the cause of all this; but not now—not now. I cannot remain any longer."

Mrs. Booker hurried to the door with an unsteady step, and an altered gait to that she entered with, and quitted the conjurer's room without waiting to hear any remark.

*　　　*　　　*　　　*　　　*　　　*　　　*

We will now turn our attention to the progress of the various schemes which were on foot, and which seemed likely enough to be productive of diverting incidents. Such a conglomeration of cross-purposes could scarcely be imagined as that which was about to occur, in which Brummel, Amelia, the young soldier, the prince, and Sheridan were concerned. Perhaps we shall see that, by an untoward event, some of the cleverness of the latter-named personage failed in producing the effect he anticipated, and recoiled upon himself.

CHAPTER XI.

SHOWS HOW THE GARDENS OF BUCKINGHAM HOUSE BECAME THE SCENE OF MANY ADVENTURES.

THE time was rapidly approaching when it would become necessary for the prince to betake himself to the garden-gate of Buckingham House in order to keep his appointment, which he was foolish enough to suppose that his rattling friend, Sherry, had made with Amelia for him.

It ought certainly to have occurred to him, as a highly probable supposition, that some trick would be played him, but certainly such did not strike him; and blinded, perchance, by his admiration of the fair country girl, he thought of nothing but the pleasure of the approaching assignation.

And not less eagerly was the evening looked for by Amelia, who had a thousand things to say to her lover, for, like many young ladies in a much more elevated sphere of life, although she had said "No" to him in the country, she had not exactly meant it.

The lady, too, in Half Moon-street was about as anxious as anybody could very well be for the time to come when she might make a trial of her fascinations, and yet as she thought to give herself a chance of winning back what never was won back yet—lost love!

But she thought it quite impossible she should plead and sue in vain to one who, in time past, had evidently pleaded and sued to her; so she really felt in very tolerable spirits, and told herself how much obliged she was to Sheridan for giving her an opportunity of attempting the recovery of a position from which she had fallen, from as great a share of demerit, as the merit that had raised her to it.

"I know his weak points," she said to her maid, as the last touch of delicate rouge was given to her face by that useful and prudent domestic, "and I will play upon them to some purpose."

"And, ma'am, if anybody can do that, you can."

"Yes, vanity—downright personal vanity—is what the man feels most of, and any one who can and will do that, will do much with him."

This was true enough in the abstract, and if she had not before been a kind friend to the individual in question, it might have succeeded, but we have more to do with action than with speculation, so we shall proceed.

It is nearly dusk, and by the garden-gate of Buckingham House appears a rather bulkish-looking individual; he takes a key from his pocket, opens a little green door, and enters—this is the prince.

No sooner is this feat accomplished, than from a doorway near at hand peeps a delightful face, half convulsed with laughter, and then retreats just in time to avoid being seen by Master George, who is cautiously peeping out for his inamorato. This is Sheridan.

But hush! who comes—whom have we here? A Hebe! yes, it is Amelia a little too soon, for the lady from Half Moon-street has not yet arrived, and George may get hold of the right person after all.

This would have been, indeed, very *mal apropos*, and for a few moments Sheridan was quite in a state of alarm lest such a thing should take place. Just, however, as, at all hazards, he was about to pounce out of his hiding-place, he saw a lady arrive, and guessed at once that it was the fair one from Half Moon-street.

"Good," he said; and then he had reason in another moment to think that it was better than good, for in her hurry she passed the little garden gate, and then turned back again, finding she had done so, so that she had all the appearance of having come from Pimlico.

This was just as Sheridan would have wished it, and when he saw, at the same moment, this little door open a short distance, and the prince look out, and, seeing the lady, then fairly emerge, and make a profound bow, he was so delighted that he almost laughed outright.

The lady affected a coyness; but Master George bowed again, and said—

"Miss, I am well aware that you have come here to meet an individual who will be most happy to see you. This way, if you please."

At these inviting words, the lady's scruples appeared to vanish, and although she seemed to tremble, as a young maiden might be supposed to do, she crossed the threshold of that private entrance to the garden of Buckingham House, which was an old-fashioned square building, which few of our readers probably remember.

At the moment Sheridan rushed to meet Amelia, who started at his sudden appearance.

"Pardon me, Miss Amelia Booker," he said, "but your lover the soldier dare not make his appearance openly here, for fear one of his officers should see him, and he has commissioned me to conduct you to him."

"Thank you, sir—oh, thank you," said Amelia, trembling, and not knowing what to do exactly; but he did not give her time to think, but hurrying her up to the little door, he tapped smartly at it.

George had got back a few paces from it when this appeal for admission was made, and with an imprecation, he turned to listen.

Then suddenly remembering his promise to Sheridan—yes, for once in a way, he did remember a promise—he hastily opened the door.

"You forgot me," whispered Sheridan. "That will do."

"D—n you."

"Thank you; doorkeepers are always unpleasant people, I believe. There be off, I have got my jewel here, and you, I suppose, have the fair Amelia?"

"Hush! not a word. Close the door—you go to the right, and I will go to the left."

"Agreed, all's right."

"And—and—Sherry——"

"Well, what?"

"If there should be any disturbance, you know—any regular riot, I shall throw it all upon you. I expect you to get me out of it."

"But how can I account for two ladies? One I might."

"Oh, nonsense—you must."

"Very good," laughed Sheridan. "I think your fair damsel is getting alarmed and suspicious; I can see her even by this faint light tremble. Ha! ha! ha!"

"But, sir," whispered Amelia, "where is Atterbury? I don't see him—oh, where is he, and where am I? I don't like all this at all, and I begin to be afeard—I do. Oh dear—oh dear!"

"Now, really, my charmer——"

"I aint your charmer, sir."

"Well, well—come this way, and I will take you to your gallant lover, who no doubt most anxiously expects you. This way—this way, Amelia, if you please—this way. I dare say he is all impatience to see you. But don't speak another word just yet, or you might be his ruin. This way. In this summer-house he ought to be."

Sheridan urged her on until they reached a little, gay, summer-house, the door of which he fastened on the inside, and then clasping one of her hands in his, he said—

"Amelia, I have that to tell you which I feel I ought at once to communicate to you, inasmuch as it most nearly concerns your happiness, and not finding your soldier lover here induces me at once to tell it. In a word, I love you."

"Sir!"

"Yes, I love—adore you, Amelia. Oh, pardon—pardon the little dramatic stratagem, by which I have been enabled to pour into your ears the tale of my affections."

"Sir!"

"You are a country girl, and probably you never heard of such affection as I feel for you. The warmth of the flame that consumes me, the—the—the——"

"Really, this is great nonsense; can it be possible that I am listening to the learned—the polite—lively Sheridan? Are you the man who was wont to set the table in a roar? Why I never heard such common-place fustian in all my life; and so you think you have perpetrated a very clever stroke of policy. Oh, silly creature! Rise, sir, from that posture of real degradation, and affected passion, I command you."

Sheridan was completely bewildered.

"What, are you the—the unsophisticated, ignorant country girl? Are you—and yet speak to me in such a tone, and use such language? Am I dreaming?"

"Better, sir, think that you dreamt you sought the dishonour of one entitled rather to the best protection of a gentleman, than be forced to own to yourself the disgrace of such a plan, conceived and attempted to be carried out in your waking moments. Oh, shame, shame! 'Tis well the shadows of night hide the conscious flush of guilt on the face of one who ought to be above petty and unworthy intrigue."

"The deuce!"

"As you please, sir. Announce or call any of your acquaintances you please."

"Then you have been only playing the part of the—the—the——"

"Coventry hoyden, in the last new farce of—'The Trickster tricked, or Sheridan outwitted.'"

"Lady—Miss Booker."

"Sir!"

"I own my defect. I beg your pardon, allow me to lead you to the gate again, and to see you clear of the place."

"Stop, sir. I have shamed you out of playing to me the part of the man of gallantry and the eprobate. Will you come out in a more worthy line?"

"As what?"

"As the sincere friend of Amelia Booker."

"With pleasure—with pleasure. Let past folly be forgotten. I was charmed with your beauty—I am now more charmed with your sense and wit, and you bestow upon me a high compliment by allowing me to call myself your friend; and the sooner you place me in the way of earning the title properly, by the performance of some act which will convince you that I am not a reprobate, the better pleased shall I be."

"Hush! what noise is that?"

"Noise? I heard nothing. What was it like? Ah, a hasty footstep, Miss Booker; we are not the only parties in the gardens to-night who will have to come to some explanation, although ours will be the most satisfactory."

No. 5.

"What do you mean?"

"Hush! do not say a word. Listen, and you will be amused, if not instructed. That is the voice of one who, by Divine Grace, will fill a throne. Is it not dignified? Ha, ha, ha!"

"The Prince of Wales!"

"Yes, yes—glorious fun, glorious fun! He has found out his mistake, and the old story of the lovers in the ' Midsummer Night's Dream' is, I expect, being acted to perfection. I would not miss this for much."

"You alarm me. What is it?"

At this moment a voice, which would no doubt have been louder but for a solitary fear of being heard by some of the domestics of the house, cried—

"D—n it, madam, am I to be kidnapped—taken by storm—tormented? D—n it! how came you here? But no matter; get you gone again as quick as you can. Somebody shall pay dearly for this."

"If he means me," said Sheridan, " and can really make me pay for it, he will be the first person who ever did make me pay for anything."

―――――――

CHAPTER XII.

THE PRINCE'S MISTAKE—ITS CONSEQUENCES.

IT was indeed the prince's voice that Sheridan and Amelia heard in the garden, and from the tone of it, it was evident to him, Sheridan, that there was considerable disquietude about the feelings, just then, of his illustrious companion.

"What ho! hilloa! Sherry, Sherry!" he cried, " where are you? Here is some abominable mistake or another."

"Who is that?" cried Amelia, is it really——"

"Hush! the prince—do not speak loud enough to be overheard."

Amelia was silent, and in a few moments the voice of the prince died away as he walked down some path of the garden which did not communicate with the place where Sheridan and the fair Amelia were.

"There," said the light-hearted Sherry, "then we are safe now. He has gone."

"Then I will go too," said Amelia, " and remember that I have your promise to assist me in the emancipation of my poor master from the state of thraldom into which I feel convinced he has fallen."

"You may rely upon me at any time; send for me when you will, you may always depend upon my most prompt attention, Amelia; and I cannot help saying that I think your uncle's case a serious one, and that he is in positive danger from his wife. But yet, let her do what she may, she must be so very cautious in doing it, that a little more caution may outwit her; however, if you will follow me, I will return to show you out of the gardens of Buckingham House, of which, by this time, although you have seen very little, I dare say you have yet seen enough."

"Oh, quite, quite," said Amelia, "quite. I leave the garden with much more confidence and pleasure than I came to it."

"No doubt."

Sheridan led the way, and, with the fair girl's arm resting in his, he conducted her to the little private entrance, which, although on the outside it was impregnable except to a key most artfully constructed, could be most easily opened on the in.

"Now, Master George," he said to himself, with a laugh, after he had placed Amelia in her right route to her home, " now, Master George, you may accuse me, as doubtless you will, of some share in your deep disappointment of to-night, but you cannot prove it, I think; so the laugh will be upon my side after all."

It will be somewhat amusing to see how the prince bore his disappointment, and accordingly, we take him up at that precise point when he thought himself so wonderfully successful, and was escorting her whom he fully believed to be Amelia Booker, to a pavilion in the gardens, after having admitted Sheridan,

"My charmer," said George. "this is indeed a pleasure."

" Oh, gracious!" said the lady, in a feigned voice, for she had been very well instructed by Sheridan in the part she had to play, "what do I hear? You are not he whom I came to meet, sir."

"Nay, do not be alarmed. I am he who loves you, at all events."

"Loves me? Oh, help! help!"

The lady certainly did cry for help, but it was in such a gentle tone that it would not have disturbed a slumbering cockchafer, and George considered that he was getting on famously.

"I know, my charmer," he said, "I know that you came here to meet a soldier—oh, how very unworthy of your love is one so low in degree as he is. I, too, am a soldier, but not one of the condition of him who is so much honoured by having your regard."

"Alarm seizes me. Oh, what can I say?"

By this time they had arrived at the summer-house to which they had been walking with considerable rapidity, and in which was a small oil lamp with a sort of hood or shade over it, that almost entirely obscured its beams, but which might be removed with ease, and then it gave a tolerable light in the small space of the pretty summer-house.

"You tremble," said the prince; "why, what a foolish creature you are, my dear; what on earth can you be afraid of, I should like to know? Come, we will see what these pretty cheeks are made of—I will throw a light upon the fairest subject in the world."

"Held, hold—do not, just yet."

"And why not just yet, pretty one? What a state of agitation you are in, to be sure; was there ever anything like it? Why you tremble like—I don't know what; really, now, really——"

And she did tremble indeed; perhaps she half repented of the step she had taken, and would have given, at that moment, something handsome to have avoided the *eclaircissement* that in a few moments must now ensue. She took one of his hands in hers—she clung to it, and she wept convulsively: this was real emotion. There was no acting now; the stake for which she played was too serious a one. It might again instal her as a royal favourite, or it might mar her for ever. t

"Oh, bear with me a moment," she said. "Do not say anything harsh to me, and do not look anything harsh at me; and repent that——"

"Repent! Repent of what? And yet surely that voice is familiar to me—I have heard i before, and yet where I cannot say. Speak again."

She could not speak for sobbing.

The prince was getting suspicious. He thought that there was something wrong, but did not know what exactly, until suddenly disengaging one hand from the clasp of her who tried to detain both, he flung the hood off the little lamp, and then by a glance he knew her.

"Good God! what brought you here?"

"Hear me—oh, hear me. You once loved me. You have cast me off, but surely some fond remembrance of the past must cling to you still. I cannot forget what we once were. Oh, George, do not put on that dreadful look—I implore you do not. Look kindly, and hear what I have to say. If any one has by the slightest word made you doubt my affection they have wronged me. You know that it was my pride, as well as my pleasure, to love you—I love you still—and shall ever do so while life remains to me. I would sooner die than think that you cared nothing for me—much sooner die, George. Oh, kill me, or say that you still think something kindly of her whom you once, I know, loved sincerely."

All this while she clung to his hand, and he could not have escaped if he would, although there can be but little doubt he would have done so if he could.

"This is too bad," he said, "this is too bad. The scoundrel Sherry has deceived me—it is too bad. Rise at once, madam, I—I have nothing to say to you—nothing whatever. Good God, how very disagreeable!"

"Nay, once more look at me, I implore you."

"Madam, I have already looked at you once too often. By whatever trick you got here, allow me to tell you that—that—at all events let me urge you to go. This supplication is useless. I—I am fickle if you like—what you like—but go at once. I have no money, or you should have some. For God's sake go away, and don't make a scene here."

"Cruel—cruel!"

"Well, well, just as you like; cruel, if you will have it so, and there's an end of t. Do go away, or positively I shall leave you here, and you will have your own explanations to make to the servants when they find you."

"And is all love, all consideration for me extinct in your heart?"

"Every portion; now you fully understand me. I am astonished at a woman of your penetration thinking that anything was to be gained by such a scene as this."

If she had been ambiguous about the words he uttered, there was no mistaking the tone of complete indifference which he used. She felt that she had made a terrible miscalculation, and that there was not the most distant hope of her fascinations having any further effect upon the volatile mind of him who once had been her most devoted admirer.

This to such a woman was a conviction that brought both despair and anger in its turn, and half crying, half threatening, she rose from her suppliant position, saying—

"Wretch! and is it thus that all my devotion is received? Is it thus that the love of a woman who can love as I have done is to be treated? You chose a scene in these gardens; I may not have another opportunity of being in them, and therefore a scene you shall have."

"Are you mad?"

"Nearly so; at all events, I must have some revenge. You cannot strike me, and here I will cling to you. Strike me off, if you can; hurt me, and my screams shall summon to the spot every one within hearing. You do not know what a desperate woman can do."

This was certainly anything but pleasant, and for a few moments Master George seemed to be absolutely panic-stricken. Well he knew that, if what was taking place were to reach the ears of the queen, she would, and very properly too, be much scandalised at the gardens of one of the royal residences being made the scene of such affairs; and, from the determined manner of his quondam favourite, it was quite evident she was serious about it.

Perhaps she gathered hope from the silence which he kept up for a few moments, and relaxed her hold of him a trifle. He seized the opportunity, and snatching away his hand, by which she principally had held him, he ran out of the summer house as if a legion of devils had been at his heels. For a moment he got a good start, for she was paralysed at the suddenness of the movement; but when she did recover, she pursued him, and perhaps never had there been such a chase in those gardens since they had been gardens.

It was a few moments after this that George had approached so near to where Sheridan and Amelia were holding their confabulation, that they heard his voice; and when he ran down a walk near at hand, which was fortunate, or else he would have pounced upon Sherry and Amelia, he was collared by one of the royal grooms, who, not knowing him in the dark, exclaimed—

"Hilloa, my fine fellow, what now?"

"Take your hands off me, you scoundrel!"

The man happened to know his voice, and was immediately all submission and apologies.

"Never mind about that," was the reply. "There's a mad woman in the gardens; find her, and turn her out, without heeding, and without repeating, what she may say. Do you understand me?"

"Perfectly, your royal highness; and if you will pardon——"

"Well, well—say no more about that. It was a mistake—say no more about it. But find the mad woman, and turn her out. Confound her! she must be somewhere close at hand; and yet I don't know. What a *mal apropos* adventure to be sure; and I shall be roasted to death by Sherry, Hill, and the others. The idea of being followed up in this way."

Muttering thus his dissatisfaction at the occurrences of the evening, George walked towards the private entrance to the garden as quickly as he could, and made his escape just two minutes after Sheridan had left with Amelia, and shown her a little way on her route to the tavern, where we shall soon have to record sayings and doings of no small importance to the due progress of our story, and the further development of Mrs. Booker's schemes.

CHAPTER XIII.

SHOWS HOW BEAU BRUMMEL MET WITH A WARM RECEPTION AT STOREY'S GATE.

It will be remembered that Sheridan had not stopped short in any of the various stages of his mischievous projects that had been suggested by the prince's desire to see Amelia Booker, but had indited a note to Brummel, which was pretty sure to get that individual to Storey's-gate, Westminster, at the appointed hour.

Tom Atterbury, the soldier, had likewise been duly informed that Brummel was there, and then about to meet Amelia, and was accordingly fired with indignation.

At the hour appointed the soldier took up his post, for he was not altogether sure but that some trick might be played him; but when he saw Beau Brummel come sauntering along with a very elegant walking cane in his hand, which ever and anon he twirled by a silk tassel, with what he, no doubt, thought ineffable grace.

"The conceited puppy," muttered the soldier. "If I was but certain now that it was Amelia he came to meet, I would soon let him know what it was to——. Oh, here he comes. What an ape-like grin upon his face to be sure! I do most certainly detest him—the civet cat—the mushroom—the thread-paper—the tailor's shew-block. Oh, I must go and say something to him, I can't stand this any longer—I'll be hanged if I can."

With this he walked up to the Beau, and said in a tone of suppressed passion which Brummel mistook for deference, as it was too dark for him to see the soldier's face sufficiently distinctly to find an index to his feelings there.

" Sir, is your name Brummel ?"

" Ah, well, suppose it is; ah, what have you got to say to me, eh, my fine fellow ?"

" I suppose you are he who is called Beau Brummel, and who is so celebrated for his great gallantry ?"

" Ah, well, suppose that too—what then ?"

" Why, sir, you have come here, I understand, to meet a young lady."

" Certainly," said Brummel. " 'Tis devilish provoking; I suppose the little dear can't get out, and you have come to tell me so, and save me the infliction of waiting. I always wait ten minutes; 'pon honour I do !"

-" How very considerate !"

" I always was to the fair; ah, bearded ruffians of men, I never wait for a moment; they wait for me. But what's the message, eh? can't she come?—what a bore—what a bore."

" A terrible bore, sir; she cannot come. But I am here to meet the man—man, do I say? no, the creature who would seduce innocence for the gratification of personal vanity, and thus I punish such a transgressor—you shall remember me."

So saying, he snatched the cane from the hand of the astonished Brummel, and began laying it about his shoulders with an energy that soon converted his lounging, listless, lolling gait into the briskest dance that human being ever executed.

An assault of such a character in so public a place as the park was not likely to be perpetrated exactly with impunity, and several people immediately rushed to the spot, and among them an officer of the guards of the same regiment that Tom Atterbury belonged to. This officer knew Brummel well by sight, and, in fact, had been introduced to him, so that he might be considered an acquaintance.

" Mr. Brummel, Mr. Brummel," he cried, " what is all this about ?"

" Murder, murder ! Ah, ah—an attempt to murder me, to stop my bringing out next week the new Brummel vest. I fully—ah, ah—expected it."

Tom Atterbury threw the cane to the ground, and respectfully saluted the officer, as he said—

" Pardon me, sir, but such is not the fact. There was no attempt at anything but what has been done, namely, a caning of this man for attempting the seduction of a young girl who was to meet him here in the park."

" Go to your barracks, sir, and consider yourself under arrest. You ought to know, if you do not, that it is a high crime and misdemeanour to be brawling in the park."

The young soldier knew that to attempt just then any justification of himself to the officer, would be to make matters a great deal worse, so he, with a respectful salute, again turned and walked off in the direction of the barracks, quite satisfied that he had done an act of retributive justice as regarded Brummel, that would be a source of pleasurable reflection, let the consequences be what they might; and he did not much dread those consequences, for it was not a military crime he had committed, nor did he think that by any ingenuity it could be tortured into one.

We shall see. We have some forebodings regarding the poor Tom Atterbury.

" Sir," said the officer to Beau Brummel, as he led him away from the crowd that was collecting, "sir, you perhaps don't recollect me, but I was introduced to you at Lord Clive's; my name is Strangeways, captain in the 1st Foot Guards."

" Ah, likely enough," said Brummel; " they introduce me to so many people."

" But sir, don't you recollect dining at Lord Clive's about a fortnight ago ?"

" Oh, very probable. My fellow puts me in a coach, and takes me somewhere to dinner every day, I think; so it's likely enough. Ah !"

" Well, sir, I have no notion of allowing a gentleman to be insulted, as you have been, with impunity, and you may depend the fellow shall suffer."

" It is a most dreadful interference with the amusements of the aristocracy, sir, that a gentleman cannot go to visit a girl, without being assaulted by some ruffian who chooses to be at all virtuous."

" A frightful state of things, Mr. Brummel; but he belongs to my regiment, although he is not in my company; so that I think I can promise you that he will be made to remember to-day as long as he lives. Here is your cane, Mr. Brummel, which I picked up for you when the fellow threw it down, and I hope that you will not consider I take too great a liberty by saying that I will call upon you to-morrow morning."

" Happy to see you; George breakfasts with me at one. As for the cane, I cannot think of touching it, after that fellow has had it in his hand. My valet always puts on a new pair of white kid gloves before he presumes to hand me my cane and hat, when I am going out. Good morning, Mr.—a—Strangeways : good morning."

"Insufferable puppy," said the officer ; "if I were not, as poor as the very devil, and panting for the perferment I may get by knowing such a donkey, he should have had another taste of the cane. I wonder now if I dare venture upon the half sort of invite I have received to call upon him in the morning at one o'clock ; I must think it over. If I can push myself into that set I shall soon get hold of a colonelcy, and that will be a pretty good reward, I take it, for putting up with a few of the puppy airs of such a man as Beau Brummel. Some say he has no influence, but others again say he has vast power, and I will not throw away a chance. If I find he is really of no use to me, I must take my revenge by picking a quarrel with him, and then either horsewhip him or shoot him."

As he spoke this to himself, this specimen of military morality strolled towards St. James's Palace, where he was on duty, and from whence he despatched a serjeant to the barracks to say that Tom Atterbury was to be considered in close confinement.

There was rather a heightened colour on the cheek of Brummel, as he made his way to his lodgings at Pimlico, and as he went, he passed very near the wall of the gardens at Buckingham House ; so near, indeed, that upon the little private entrance suddenly opening, and a person rushing out with great speed, he was nearly knocked down, and as it was, his hat was thrown from his head.

This person who came out with such vehemence was a woman, and no other than the fair lady who had made so very unsuccessful an effort to call up the quenched sensibilities of the prince.

"D—n it," said Brummel, for once speaking in a natural tone of voice ; "I think there's a design upon my life to-night. Do you want to murder me, madam ?"

"Get out of my way, fool," cried the indignant lady, and she walked on, without even look-ing to see whose equilibrium it was she had so nearly destroyed.

Brummel looked carefully around him to see if there was anybody in sight before he conde-scended to stoop to pick up his hat, for had there been any human eyes to see him commit such an act of positive humiliation, he would have fainted before he would have perpetrated it.   Then as he placed the discomfited beaver upon his head, he muttered—

" Daned—my hat knocked off—called a fool—and all in one night. Humph—humph—humph I'll know why I am to be thus persecuted."

As he spoke, he with an angry gesture took up a stone and hammered upon the panel of the little door through which the lady had emerged, but no one answered him.   Fancying, however, that it was loose, he gave it a violent push, but that had no effect ; so he retreated a step, and then flung himself against it with all his force, and, unfortunately for him, did that just at the moment that the groom who had discharged the lady, opened it, to see if she was fairly gone, and the consequence was that Brummel rolled in head over heels, upsetting the groom like a battering ram.

A fight immediately ensued, and such was the uproar, that several servants came running to the spot with flambeaux, which when Brummel perceived—for he dreaded nothing so much as being the hero of a ridiculous adventure—he scrambled to his feet, and dealing the groom a blow which prevented him from stopping him at the moment, he darted through the open door-way.

No wonder that when he got home, the exquisite fainted away, and had to have a bath of scented tepid water to recover his serenity of nerve.

CHAPTER XIV.

THE DANGER OF MR. BOOKER.—THE PANACEA FOR CUTS AND WOUNDS.

UNHAPPY Booker ! The look of calm contentment which used to shine upon his face before he married had completely vanished. Alas ! he had, indeed, strangely altered. His old friends began scarcely to know him again. It was evident that some mental disquietude was wearing poor Booker to the grave, and that without any machinations at all of his wife, he would soon join the other husbands in another, and what we sincerely hope is a considerably better, world. It cannot very well be a worse, that's a comfort !

When he was alone, he would sigh and groan in a manner that would have melted the most obdurate heart, but it was only in the presence of his wife that he put on an appearance of simulated gaiety, which certainly sat uneasily upon him.

He evidently began to regard her with great terror, and if he were discoursing with any one in the bar parlour, and heard or fancied he heard her coming, he would cry " Hush !" and sud-denly change the subject.

What a state of thraldom for the once gay Booker—quietly gay, we mean—that gaiety of the heart which shines out of every lineament of the face, and is as quiet as deep-rooted grief; but, oh, how very different a feeling! Oh, how came you, Booker, with your pleasant little income that provided so nicely for all your wants, to marry any widow in the world—you, a staid, steady, serious man? Bah! Booker, you, at least, ought to have known better."

But somehow or another caution is lost or forgotten when a woman's in the case, and Mrs. Mortimer having made up her mind that she would be Mrs. Booker, became Mrs. Booker, without, we suppose, the victim having power to prevent the fascinating alliance.

"My dear," she said to him, on the very morning after the meeting had taken place between Amelia and Sheridan in the gardens of Buckingham House, "my dear, I think that now and then you ought certainly to invite your old friends to come and see you."

"Old friends?" groaned Booker.

"Yes, why not? You know we are most peculiarly situated in that respect, owing to keeping a tavern; it can scarcely ever happen that a visitor can put us out of our way, or be any encumbrance. There is, as you very well know, always a good larder, and, of course, a good cellar."

"Yes yes—oh, yes!"

"Then, I say, my dear, that it would give me sincere pleasure to see some of your bachelor friends. Suppose now, you invite one or two to supper."

"Yes, good God!" said Booker in an abstracted way. "Oh, what an ass!"

"Why, what are you talking about? Are you dreaming?"

Mr. Booker gave a start, and in good sober truth he was wandering a little, and the mention of his bachelor friends had probably induced the strong impression of opinion he had given utterance to of his own folly. It was quite clear that poor Booker was each day getting more and more unequal to battling with the circumstances that surrounded him, and that, what with doubts, and what with fears, his mind was getting seriously affected —a state of things he was shewing by abstraction.

In some people it would have been violence.

"What do you say to my proposal?" inquired his wife, after a pause of a few minutes' duration.

"Oh, yes, certainly—I'll invite Thompson."

"Do so, and I will have a nice little inviting supper ready by ten o'clock for you both; and we shall, no doubt, enjoy ourselves amazingly."

"No doubt—no doubt."

Mr. Booker sat down, and wrote a note to his old friend Thompson, in which he invited him to supper in civil terms, without the slightest hint of his continued unhappiness; and it was well he did not put anything in the letter that was at all inimical to Mrs. Booker, for the moment she saw him finish the letter, by appending his signature to the foot, she snatched it from before him, saying—

"I'll read it for you;" and then she read it.

"Thank God," thought Booker, "I have said nothing about her!" and Mrs. Booker smiled approval of the contents of the epistle, which she sealed with a seal of her own, on which were the words, "I bide my time," by way of a motto; and, when Booker saw them, he said—

"Dear me, what an odd motto! What does it mean?"

"I don't know," said Mrs. Booker, "really;" and, as she said this with all the *nonchalence* in the world, it really seemed as if she did not know; and Booker, with a groan, again relapsed into a state of abstraction.

A short time after this, Amelia came in, and sat down by him in silence; but after a time she said—

"Uncle, I am quite sure you are not so happy as you would fain induce me to believe you are. What is it that torments you? Cannot you confide in me? Surely you know that you may, and that I am bound to you by all the ties of affection and consanguinity!"

Booker stared at her.

"You need not be afraid to speak freely," she added. "Mrs. Booker is not in the house at present, and it is better that you should tell me what you really think, than suffer me perhaps to make some mistake, owing to trying to guess your feelings.

Booker stared at her again. "Why, Amelia," he said, "is this you? I—I thought you were next door to a fool."

Amelia laughed, as she replied—

"Perhaps I was; but that is no reason why I should love my neighbours sufficiently to be a fool myself."

"No, girl, no, girl, certainly; I am wretched—wretched! but for God's sake do not let her—my wife, I mean—suspect that I have said as much; but I am, for all that, wretched, most wretched. Oh, Amelia, never marry a widow who has had half a dozen husbands beforehand."

" I, uncle, why what do you mean ?"

" Oh, oh, of course ; sometimes I really don't know what I am saying, my dear,—excuse me I, was only wandering a little, that's all."

" A little, uncle, I think you were wandering a great deal. But I have got something to tell you, that it is important you should listen to, and thoroughly understand, and never forget for a single moment."

" I will attend to you. What is it you wish to say, my dear ? hush ! is that her coming ?"

" No, it's only Maria. What I want to say to you, uncle, is just this, never take anything in the shape of medicine from your wife ; whatever you do, mind you don't ever complain of indis- position, or you may perhaps find it very difficult to avoid taking something that may not do you any good."

" Good God ! you don't suspect——"

" What ?"

" That she would poison me. You don't surely think, Amelia, that she poisoned Mortimer, Lee Luton, Fiddler, Brown, and Green ? Oh, good God !"

" I suspect nothing, uncle ; I only ask you to be careful. You have disposed of your whole income, have you not, to her ?"

" Yes, in a life assurance, which she made me effect ; and I have made an agreement that forces me to keep up the premium, and that swallows up certainly my whole income."

" Did not that open your eyes ?"

"To what ?"

" Hush, she comes. Talk upon some indifferent subject to her, but do not forget what I have been saying to you, uncle : I will tell you more another opportunity,—I am not exactly the foolish ignorant country girl I seemed to be, but I will still be such to Mrs. Booker, so keep my secret."

" I will, I will."

Mrs. Booker made her appearance, and looked sharply at her husband as she said, " What ails you ?"

" Nothing, nothing at all," said Booker.

" Ah," said Amelia, " he don't like to tell, but he has promised me—haven't you, uncle ?— that he would by degrees leave off smoking his pipe up stairs ; for there is not a bedroom in the place, nor an article of my clothes, let me shut them up in my drawers ever so tight, that don't smell of tobacco smoke."

" Yes," said Booker, much relieved at this suggestion of Amelia's, " yes, I will make the attempt, but as I was only just now saying, my dear, before you came in, smoking is one of those habits which it is very difficult indeed to break oneself of."

" Oh, is that all ? "

" Quite all, my dear—quite, I assure you it was nothing else."

" Well, then, my dear Mr. Booker, I can only say that I think Amelia is too particular. If it is any enjoyment to you to smoke your pipe, and that it is so I am tolerably well assured, you go on smoking it. Heaven forbid that any interference should be given to your pleasures."

" Thank you—thank you."

" And now what would you like to give to your friend Thompson for his supper to-night ? I suppose he will be sure to come."

" Anything you like, my dear. Thompson certainly is a man that is fond of anything nice and relishing ; but I will leave it entirely to you, my dear, being quite convinced that then it will be all right. Oh, what an ass!"

" What do you mean, Mr. B——, by that expression?"

" Eh ?" cried Booker, who had suddenly fallen into one of his fits of abstraction. " Eh ? what did I say ?"

" Well, well—it's no matter. But it sounds foolish. However, we will say nothing about it, and, I dare say, we shall pass a very pleasant evening, indeed, together, for I am sure any friend of yours, Mr. B—— will be doubly and trebly welcome to me at any time."

" She is, after all, a charming woman!" thought Booker.

CHAPTER XV.

THE SUPPER.—AND HOW MR. BOOKER GOT A CUT FINGER.—SHERIDAN'S IMPERTINENCE.

A NOTE came in due course from Mr. Thompson, to say that he would be abundantly happy to sup with Mr. and Mrs. Booker, and would be at the Wheatsheaf at the hour appointed ; and being a very punctual man, he, just as the neighbouring clocks, by tolerably unanimous consent, agreed that it was ten, made his appearance.

And most truly had Mrs. Booker done justice to the old friend of her husband, in the supper she had caused to be prepared for the occasion.   It consisted of some most enticing luxuries, and would have tempted even an anchorite.

The good St. Anthony among all his temptations had not a rich, unctuous supper offered to him, or surely he would have yielded, and just picked a little bit.

And Mrs. Booker had herself been into the kitchen, and had given the last finishing, artistic touch to the cooking, so that everything was done to a turn, and when the table was laid, and even

No. 6.

before the covers were removed, there arose from all sorts of crevices and corners such a grateful perfume that Mr. Thompson sniffed and sniffed again, and whispered to Booker,—

"I say, after all, we cannot do things in this sort of way, we old fellows of bachelors, can we?"

"Oh dear no," said Booker. "Pray sit down."

Suddenly, just as the guest was seating himself, there arose quite a clamour outside the room, and the voice of Maria was heard saying,—

"No, indeed, sir. You cannot go in. My mistress has got company in the bar-parlour, and surely you would not be so unpolite as to intrude. At any other time, sir, any customer of the house and gentleman like yourself can always walk in."

"Oh, stuff!" said a half-tipsy voice; "stuff and nonsense. If she has company, I shall be an acquisition. I don't want any more wine, for I have had my three bottles of claret, and that's quite enough. Go, my dear, and say to your charming mistress that Mr. Sheridan presents his compliments, and will sup with her to-night."

"Mr. who?" said Thompson.

A shade of displeasure passed across the features of Mrs. Booker, and she half rose from her seat as she said, "It's Sheridan; he often comes to the house, but I really cannot allow it to be taken by storm in this kind of way. Oh no—I——"

"Madam," said Sheridan, as he entered the room, having overcome the resistance of Maria, "madam, I beg of you to be seated. 'Tis strange, madam, but when I think of female beauty and excellence, the name of Mrs. Mortimer rings in my very ears like a peal of music. Do not let me disturb you, ladies, and you, sir, Mr. Booker, I presume, you will find me no trouble. What a charming day we have had, Mrs. Booker, if it had not been for the wind which has blown a gale, and the rain which has come down incessantly. What, ho! Who waits? Remove the covers."

"But, sir——"

"Thank you, madam, any seat will do for me. Don't move, Booker; I will take the bottom of the table, and face your charming wife. Ah! madam, I am seldom so happy."

Maria tripped into the room and began to remove the covers, and Mrs. Booker whispered to her,—

"Why did you let him in? You see, now, there is no getting rid of him."

"Oh, ma'am, I couldn't help it; he began kissing me so furiously—I was forced to let him in."

"Now this is enjoyment," exclaimed Sheridan, "here we are, all choice spirits, and tiled, so that we may say anything we like; and the savoury fumes of the supper are enough to awaken an appetite in the jaws of Death itself."

Mrs. Booker said nothing, but vexation was visible upon her countenance. As for Thompson, he stared with his mouth wide open; but at length whispered to Booker,—

"You don't mean to say that's *the* Sheridan?"

"Oh, yes; I believe so. Oh dear me! Do you know, Thompson, I feel quite like a man in a dream."

The plates were filled, the rich wine sparkled in the glasses, and Sheridan said so many clever and complimentary things to Mrs. Booker, that she, not having any reason to suppose his presence there was anything but a new frolic, began to be reconciled to it, and to be pleased enough now and then to smile in spite of herself. When did that prince of boon companions fail to make himself welcome, and with quips and cranks and wreathed smiles, to

"Set the table in a roar,"

Anecdote upon anecdote flowed from his lips, and almost every remark that he made was epigrammatic. The supper was getting on amazingly. Booker looked cheerful, and lost some of his abstraction, while Thompson was quite delighted, although he had been almost twenty times stopped by Sheridan in the telling of the only anecdote he knew, just as he was coming to the point of it, too.

A pheasant was placed before Mrs. Booker to carve.

"Shall I relieve you, madam," said Sheridan.

"No, sir, I thank you. I think I can manage tolerably; and I ought to be able to do so."

This was said with one of her most bewitching smiles, and she commenced manipulating the pheasant with evident skill. But as people say, " accidents will happen in the best regulated families," and the most accomplished carver will now and then make a slip—Mrs. Booker made one upon this occasion, and not only sent a leg of the bird into the lap of Mr. Booker, who sat next to her, but, *accidentally*, just touched his hand with the blade of the carving knife, and inflicted a gash upon it which bled freely.

"Oh, how very awkward of me," said the lady.

"Oh, no, no," said Booker, "it's—it's of very little consequence. Only a slight cut—a very slight cut, indeed."

"I shall never forgive myself."

"Who would not willingly," said Sheridan, "pay such a price as that if it were but for the pleasure of hearing you, madam, so charmingly express sympathy?"

"You are very kind, Mr. Sheridan, to say so; but still it was awkward of me, and if I had not a sovereign cure for all cuts and wounds, I should feel very unhappy about it."

"And that cure, madam, is a glance from those sparkling eyes!"

"No, sir, it is something, I am happy to say, that is much more to the purpose, although not quite so poetical. I will get some drops, which, placed upon a small piece of linen, which is then to be wrapped round the wound, will have the most wonderful healing effect."

She was on the point of rising; but Sheridan sprung to his feet, and was at her side in a moment, as he said,—

"No, madam—no, no."

"What do you mean, sir?"

"I mean merely that even if any of our heads were cut off, it is contrary to my religion ever to allow the lady of the house to leave the table until the cloth is removed. I dare say, Booker, you can wait."

"Oh, yes—yes."

"But, Mr. Sheridan, I have not to leave the room, for the drops I want are in a little bottle in yonder bureau."

"Of which, madam, you will then give me the key. Thank you, I see you have it in your hand; and I will get the panacea for cuts and wounds."

As he spoke, he twitched the key of the bureau from the hands of Mrs. Booker, and went towards the antique-looking piece of furniture.

"Really," said Mrs. Booker, "this is too bad."

"Oh, let him have his own way, my dear," said Booker, "he is so very amusing."

"Now, madam," cried Sheridan, when he had opened the bureau, and kept his back towards the lady so that she could not see what he was about. "I have torn a piece off my own handkerchief, with which to bind up the wound of our friend Booker. Is this the bottle?"

"Oh, no," said Mrs. Booker, as he suddenly turned and showed her a bottle. "That's a pickle bottle. I will come."

"Now, aunt, don't," said Amelia, gently detaining Mrs. Booker in her chair. "Don't, aunt, don't. Let him have his own way, pray. He is so very amusing a gentleman. Is he not, Mr. Thompson?"

"Yes, indeed. I beg you will not stir, madam. Recollect it is *the* Sheridan."

"God bless me!" said Booker, "how my finger bleeds to be sure."

"It's a small, green bottle, up in the right hand corner," said Mrs. Booker, with a tone of vexation.

"Then, this is it," said Sheridan, turning.

"Yes, yes. Place four or five drops upon the handkerchief, and then bring it to me, and I will bind up the finger."

"Certainly, madam, certainly."

In about a minute Sheridan came with the piece of his handkerchief that he had with such wonderful politeness torn off, tolerably well saturated with some liquid. He gave it to Mrs. Booker, who was at great pains to bind it round the finger of her husband that had been cut, pressing almost painfully into the wound that portion of the handkerchief which had been saturated with the mysterious and wonderful liquid in the little green bottle.

Mr. Booker shrunk a little, but, after a few moments, she tied up his hand, saying, in rather a marked manner,—

"That will completely suffice. I am satisfied."

"And I," said Sheridan, as he closed the bureau, and, after locking it, returned the key to her.

"And I," said Amelia, for it was really a bad cut. "How does it feel, uncle?"

"Better, I think. But it has made me a little faint. I will take a glass of wine, if you please."

Mrs. Booker poured the wine out for him, and he quaffed it off; after which, the whole incident appeared to be forgotten, and the little party began to enjoy itself amazingly until about one in the morning, when Sheridan rose, and said, with an air of great gallantry and devotion, towards Mrs. Booker,—

"It is with inexpressible grief that I am now obliged to tear myself away from this pleasant and, to me, most delightful company."

"Oh, don't go," said Booker.

"Do stay, sir," cried Thompson. "It aint every day that one can get *the* Sheridan to supper with them."

Amelia looked beseechingly, and so did Mrs. Booker, but Sheridan shook his head.

"My fate, not my inclination, drags me away," he said. "I have an appointment at two with one who does not like to be played with, and, as I really pledged my word, I must go."

"He means the prince," whispered Thompson to Amelia.

"La!" she said, assuming a foolish look.

"Pho!" thought Thompson, "the girl's a goose."

"Yes," added Sheridan, as he took his hat from a side table, "I must go, and so, Mrs. Booker, with my best acknowledgments for the pleasure your society has afforded, and a hope that we may soon meet again under most interesting circumstances, allow me to bid you farewell."

So saying, he bowed himself out, and with him certainly seemed to go all the wit, all the pleasantry, and all the life and spirit of the little party. Truly, they found that this sparkling but erratic genius was like Falstaff in one particular, not only witty himself, but the cause of wit in others.

In another half hour the party broke up.

Thompson went home much pleased with Mrs. Booker, and she did not seem to be at all disappointed at anything that had happened during the evening, but several times she was heard by Maria to ask Mr. Booker how he felt, and when he said, "Pretty well," she did seem a little surprised.

Amelia was very thoughtful, and after she had gone to bed, or rather to her bedroom, Maria, upon having to go into her room on some errand, found her resting her head upon her hands, and sobbing as if her heart would break.

"Oh, miss, what is the matter?" exclaimed Maria.

"Nothing, nothing," replied Amelia. "Do not say you saw me thus, Maria, if you please. It is only the—the excitement of the evening. Nothing else, I assure you."

"Well, miss, of course I shall not mention it, as you don't wish. But isn't Mr. Sheridan a funny man? Oh, he is enough to make anybody laugh. I can't think what made him so anxious to sup here to-night, but he was so."

"No doubt merely for a frolic, Maria. That was all. Good night—good night."

"Good night, miss. I am tired enough, to be sure, and there goes two o'clock."

CHAPTER XVI.

SHOWS HOW A SKILFUL CHEMIST MADE A DISCOVERY.

"HURRAH! hurrah! Ha, ha, ha! That's good, my lord—you too, Clive—and you too, Hill, have said a few good things to-night; but where the deuce can Sherry be all this time?"

These words were uttered by the prince, between one and two in the morning, at a celebrated hotel, now no more, close to Pall Mall, where he and some boon companions had been supping.

"You all remember, no doubt," replied one, "that Sherry said he was going to sup with somebody's wife, and would not be here until two."

"Ah," said George, "he did say something about it, to be sure."

"By-the-by," said Colonel Hill, "what's this gossiping story going about, concerning a certain fair lady being turned out of Buckingham House gardens, and nearly upsetting Brummel, who was there accidentally, or on purpose, nobody knows which."

"Curse the story!" said George, with a frown,

"I say, Hill," whispered Clive, "don't you know that that's ticklish ground you have been treading on?"

"Not I, by Jove!"

"Then it is; I will tell you more at large hereafter. It's a devilish sore place just now, for the prince has had a desperate row with Sherry about it, who, however, put on such a face of innocence———"

"No whispering, no whispering!" cried George. "All whisperers are fined a pint of claret each, and made to drink it off at a draught."

"I'm done, I'm done. But who is this? I hear a footstep, and

"By the pricking of my thumbs,
Something wicked this way comes."

"Then it's Sheridan, without a doubt. Ah, yes, to be sure. Better late than never. But gentlemen, look all—look, was ever the king of all good fellows so lugubrious before? Oh!

rare sport, Sherry is out of sorts—is it a pain in the epigastric region—or have you just, in a fit of insanity, paid somebody?"

Sheridan did look gloomy, and when he sat down, there was a flush of excitement upon his face. He tossed off a bumper of the first wine that came to hand, without saying a word, and then drawing a long breath, he said,—

"Good fellows, do you think that at this time of night, or rather of the morning, you can all of you be serious and sober enough to keep a secret, and to enter into real serious business?"

"The end of the world is come," said one.

"Or the millennium," said another.

"Oh, that's the same thing. But I devoutly believe in both of them, since Sherry is serious."

"Ah," said Sheridan, as he rose, "I am sorry to say, I see it will not do. Don't let me be any hindrance to you; but as I really have something to do besides enjoying myself before I sleep, I must leave you."

There was now a look of blank surprise upon every face, and George said,—

"You may or you may not be serious, Sherry, for all I know. But if you are, you may count upon us, of course. Just say what you have to say. We have taken very little, and are none of us out of order."

"Hear, hear, hear!" cried the others.

"Then, listen to me," said Sheridan, as he resumed his seat,—"listen to me, and I think you will be inclined to say that what I have now to tell you is sufficiently curious."

"Attention, attention," said the prince. "Now, Sherry, begin. Leave off those damnable faces, and begin at the beginning. We are most unquestionably all attention."

"Well," he commenced, "you will no doubt all recollect that you had abundance of laughing at me on account of my persisting in the story about the ghosts of all Mrs. Mortimer's husbands coming to me when I set up one night in the haunted room of the tavern she certainly keeps so well."

"Good—yes, yes."

"What I have now to relate to you treads hard upon the heels, in a confirmatary manner, of that fact, for fact it was, I am convinced. You must know then that these spectres each had something to say about a cut finger, and as to-night I ascertained from a good friend of mine there was to be a little supper party at the tavern, I resolved to be present from a feeling that something would happen of an interesting character."

"The good friend, gentlemen, is Maria, the pretty barmaid," said Hill, "and I can tell you ———"

"Well, well, you can lie away, you know, some other time," said Sheridan; "let me tell my story now, will you."

"Did you say lie?"

"Yes, lie under false impressions, I was going to add."

"Oh, very well."

There was a roar of laughing, and Colonel Hill was condemned to drink off a pint of claret for getting angry, which he did with a very bad grace, for the landlord of the house was privately told to put as much red ink in it as he could find in the house to do so with.

"To resume then," said Sheridan.

"Ah, get on—get on. I am really getting interested," said George. "I'm sure we shall be entertained, so get on, Sherry, will you, at once, there's a good fellow."

"I will, but *imprimis*, there are no more ghosts in my narration. Well, then, I went to the supper an uninvited, and at first an unwelcome-enough guest; but, notwithstanding I am the most modest man in the world, I did, by a little gentle perseverance, succeed in pushing my way."

"Oh! oh! oh! Hear—hear!"

There were present Mr. and Mrs. Booker, Amelia, the niece of old Booker, and a Mr. Thompson, who was determined always to speak of me with an impersonal pronoun, but that is by the way. The supper passed off very well until Mrs. Booker had a pheasant to cut up, and then, in the most unaccountable manner, and yet in a seemingly natural way, she gave her husband's finger a slash with the carving knife. The ghosts had all spoken of the same thing. Well, gentlemen, of course that might be a mere coincidence, for all I know, but the female Booker then said she had a panacea for cuts and wounds in the shape of a bottle of wonderful drops. It is needless to trouble you with how I got possession of the drops without exciting her suspicions, but here is the bottle."

As he spoke, he produced a small green bottle, and it was passed round from one to the other.

"But what do you suppose it to be?" said the prince.

"I don't know. But we have all heard of poisons of so subtle a nature, that a very small portion of them introduced into the system through a wound will vitiate the whole mass of blood, and produce death from apparently quite inexplicable causes."

"By Heaven, Sherry, you have hit it."

"I fear so. And now, gentlemen, what do you you say to the ghosts?"

There was a silence, which was at last broken by Hill, saying,—

"For my part if the affair turns out as it looks now likely to to do, I shall not be in the mood to laugh at such matters again as long as I live."

"Then," said Sheridan, with a gravity that made them expect something terribly grave, "the more fool you."

"Confound you! what do you mean?"

"Why, that this ghost affair may be true, and you may hear one hundred others that are but the air-drawn fancies of a sickly brain; and after all, joking apart, it is of course possible that in a dream the information may have been given to me by the seeming agency of apparitions, when, in reality, there were none."

"True, true!" said Clive.

"There have been some most remarkable instances of persons having had dreams which have most distinctly shadowed forth events that either have happened or are to happen. And who shall say but this is one of them?"

"Well, but," said the prince, "if you had any suspicions that the bottle contained poison, I hope you did not let poor Booker have any of it."

"No, I managed that. All he had was a piece of my handkerchief, which I dipped in a water glass, that was upon the table, previous to my rising from it, to possess myself of the bottle."

"And what do you mean to do?"

"I have not decided. It may be all nothing, and resolve itself into the fact of my having had a strange dream, that happened, in one of its particulars, to come true. But here is the proof."

"I understand you. If that be poison——"

"Then is Widow Mortimer the murderess of all her husbands, and a perfect monster in human form."

They all rose from their seats with some excitement as these words were pronounced, and the prince said,—

"Gentlemen, this grows serious."

"Yes," said Clive, "if, after all, it be not one of Sherry's elaborate jokes. I mistrust him."

"What can I say," said Sheridan, "to convince you? I know that, like the boy in the fable, I have amused myself by calling wolf until you will not believe me; but, on my honour as a gentleman, this is no jest."

"I'm satisfied."

"And I," said Colonel Hill. "I propose that we go at once and knock up Griffiths, the old chemist, in St. James's-street, than whom I have heard say that there is not a better in the whole of Europe. We will get his opinion about the contents of the bottle."

"Will not to-morrow be better?" said the prince. "He will think it only a joke at this hour, you may depend."

"I think," said Sheridan, "we can convince him to the contrary of that. I have made up my mind to place this bottle with its contents in the hands of some scientific man before I sleep, and Griffiths, who is a rough spoken fellow, but who has a high character as a chemist, will do very well. So come on."

It was striking three when the four of them, without any of the usual noise, sallied forth from the tavern in Pall-mall, and walked along tolerably orderly towards St. James's-street, for the purpose of consulting the old chemist who had been mentioned, and who certainly fully deserved the reputation he had.

It was but a small shop, Mr. Griffiths', for at that time the spirit of plate glass and gilding had not by any means made the way it has now; and when the little party halted at it, there was not another soul to be seen in St. James's-street, for the watchman was fast asleep in his box, at the corner, and even the late taverns had vomited forth all of their visitors who had any intention of going home at all, or had any home to go to.

"Ring him," said the prince; "these physical people are used to that, you know."

"Ah, to be sure," replied Hill. "But don't crack any joke with him, when he puts his head out of window now, or else of course he won't come down."

"Certainly not," said Sheridan, "I pray you will let me speak to him, for I am really anxious upon the subject."

"Yes, let him—let him," said the prince; "I am getting anxious likewise."

Sheridan himself rung the night-bell at the chemist's long and loudly, and then they all got out into the middle of the road to look up at the windows, to see at which one old Griffiths would make his appearance.

They had not to wait long, for accustomed as he was to nocturnal summonses, the old man soon showed himself, only they wondered that he opened it to its full extent.

"Well," he cried, "what the devil is it now?"

"Sir," said Sheridan, "we want to speak to you for a moment or two on very particular business, if you will favour us by coming down at once."

CHAPTER XVII.

THE DOCTOR'S OPINION.—THE RUINED NOBLEMAN.

THERE was a pause of a few moments' duration, after Sheridan thus spoke, and then the chemist said,—

"Sir, I think I know you. Are you Mr. Sheridan?"

'I am, Mr. Griffiths; and now that you do know me, I hope you will come down at once, as I have something of great importance indeed, and which I wish to say before I retire to rest."

The old man disappeared from the window, no doubt, as they thought, to come down and admit them, and they collected in a little group together, just by the curb-stone of the pavement, talking about Widow Mortimer and the mysterious little green bottle.

"I declare for my own part," said the prince, "that it's the most interesting adventure I have had for a long time."

"Yes," added Clive, "and there is still a wide field for conjecture yet, as to how it will end."

"Is there?" said a voice from above. "Now, you know how it will end, and that will teach you to come playing your mad tricks upon me again."

Even as the words were uttered, and before there was any time to get out of the way, slouch came a powerful cataract of soot and water, from the window at which the chemist had first shown himself; and they found, to their dismay, they had each had a liberal share of it, although the prince was in the worst plight, and proportionably angry.

"There, damn it," he said; "that all comes of Sheridan's bad character. The moment he was known, a joke was at once suspected, and behold the consequences."

"Confound the old fool," muttered Sheridan; "I suppose if any one was to be dying, I should not be able to get a doctor for them. That's rather too bad. What the deuce is all this riot about?"

As he spoke, there came a motley collection of boys, and a couple of men, dragging along a small fire engine, which was lumbering along the pavement, making uproar enough to awaken the whole parish.

"Where have you been," said Sheridan; "is there a fire?"

"There was an alarm, sir, but it was out when we got there," said one of them despondingly; "and here we are, gentlemen, all ready, with a nozzle screwed on to the hose, and an engine full of water, to soften the tubes to keep them from cracking, and leaking, and we haven't had a fire for five weeks: what do you think of that, gentlemen, for a piece o' aggravation?"

"Dreadful," said Sheridan, as he took hold of the mouthpiece of the engine and directed it against old Griffiths' window. "Ring the doctor's bell some of you, and then pump away like madmen, and it will be a couple of guineas among you. Here is glorious revenge, who says Providence is not good to us now, I should like to know;—ring away, you devils, and pump away Now for it,—now for it. Old Griffiths, I think, when I do come again, you will recollect me, rather!"

"I think he will, sir," said one of the engine men, as he looked on from the opposite side of the way. "Of course, sir, if there's any row about this, you know you did it, while I happened to be looking opposite."

"Admirable! admirable! You would make a first-rate diplomatist, my friend; and now that all the dirty water is expended that you keep in your engine, I would advise you to be off as fast as you can. Hill, lend me a guinea, will you, for a little time?"

Colonel Hill shook his head as he handed the coin to Sheridan, who passed it on to the man, saying,—

"There, my friend, don't you, now, ever be one of those who raise a clamour against me, and say that Sheridan never pays anybody anything."

" Sheridan, sir ! Lord bless me, sir, are you Mr. Sheridan ?"

" Be off with you, will you ? be off !"

" Look out !" said George, suddenly, as he darted into a doorway. " Look out ! Every one for himself. There's danger."

Sheridan looked up to the chemist's window, and in the dim night light he saw that enraged individual with something in his hand that looked amazingly like a blunderbuss. It was astonishing to see the effect this had upon the whole party. In another minute St. James's-street was clear.

" The scoundrels," muttered the chemist, as he shut his window; " I should have liked to give them a charge of shot."

" What am I to do ?" sobbed his wife; " I'm swimming about in the bed. I knew if you threw a jug of water out upon people, they would throw a mug-full in some night."

" A mug-full ! It would be a most alarming mug to hold all the water they pumped in at the window. I only wonder where the devil they got the engine so opportunely—but I suppose it was all a planned thing, the scoundrels."

The party, consisting of Sheridan and his associates, soon found a tavern, into which they made their way ; and, being well known, they were accommodated with supper and wines, being the third time that night that they had partaken of that meal.

It was not until the dawn of morning that they separated, and retired to sleep somewhere. Sheridan remained at the tavern, with a determination to get what repose he could, and then in the morning—that is to say, his morning, about two o'clock in the day—persevere in getting of the chemist in St. James's-street an analysis of the contents of the green bottle which he had brought from Mrs. Booker's bureau, and which, during all the subsequent proceedings of that night, he had taken great care of.

The morning was bright and beautiful, and it actually had not struck one o'clock when Sheridan, having invigorated himself with a good breakfast, and a glass or two of light Rhenish wine to give tone to his stomach, sallied out to call upon Mr. Griffiths, the chemist.

Any other man would, certainly, with a recollection of the preceding night's adventure, have rather preferred going somewhere else, or at all events if that would not have answered his purpose, he would have felt a little degree of nervousness and apprehension ; but not so was it with Sheridan. He walked into the shop with all the coolness in the world, and addressing a boy who was behind the counter, he said,—

" Is your master within ?"

" Yes, sir."

" Then tell him that Mr. Sheridan wants to see him upon the same business he came about last."

" Certainly, sir; pray take a seat," said the boy ; and away he went upon his errand to a laboratory that was at the back of the premises, where Mr. Griffiths made up under his own superintendence chemical compounds for use in his shop.

Not above half a minute certainly could have elapsed from the boy leaving the shop to the return of the chemist, whose face was all of a glow with indignation at what he considered the cool effrontery of Sheridan, and certainly it did look very like it.

" Sir," he said, " I really should have thought, after what passed last night, that I should have been spared the pain of seeing you, and being compelled to tell you that you are no gentleman, Mr. Sheridan. Your conduct last night was infamous—most infamous, sir."

" What do you mean ?" said Sheridan, assuming an aspect of great indignation likewise. " What do you mean, sir ? I have come in this morning to know if you have any apology to offer for your most unwarrantable conduct of last night. I can hardly conceive that any man in his senses would behave as you behaved, sir. Good God! what are you in such a business as yours for, if you are to refuse custom, and throw water—cold water—upon your best friends ?"

" Now this is assurance," said the chemist. " I'll go to a police-office at once."

" What, to proclaim that you made a mistake, and that you turned away people who came to you upon *bona fide* business, just because you fancied it might be a joke ! I can tell you, sir, that the business I came upon was most important. Look at that."

Sheridan handed the little green bottle to the old man, who, smothering all his indignation, habitually put it to his nose to smell its contents.

" What is it ?" he said.

" That, sir, I cannot tell you. But that was why I came to you last night. Not knowing the contents of that bottle, but having some horrible suspicions concerning it, I came as any one naturally would, to the most eminent practical chemist that London could afford, and got a jug of water in my face for my pains. Oh, Mr. Griffiths, you ought to have more temper, sir. You ought, indeed."

"Well—but—but——"

"Oh, don't attempt to excuse yourself, sir. I am the victim, as usual."

"Well, really, if I had known that—that—you—you came upon any legitimate errand, I really would have got up at once; but, you know, Mr. Sheridan, that you have a very so-so sort of reputation, and, after all, if I threw a quart of water upon you, you threw about six gallons upon me."

"Well, sir, we will let that pass. I am not a vindictive man. I forgive and forget easily. Will you find out what that bottle contains, and call upon me at the Mitre Tavern, in Piccadilly, this evening, and let me know."

Oh, certainly, sir, certainly. At what time?"

"About ten, I think, will do; but be careful not to mention the affair to any one, for more lives than one hang upon your opinion, Mr. Griffiths. 'Tis, I assure you, an extremely serious affair."

"Depend upon me, sir."

Sheridan took his leave of the worthy chemist, who was really, now that the matter had assumed the shape of actual business, sorry that he had given his visitors of the preceding evening such a reception as he had; but he soon forgot all about that as he became absorbed in an analysis of the contents of the mysterious green bottle.

No 7.

Habitually silent and cautious, he said nothing to his assistant, but pursued a careful examination of one half of the liquid, locking up the other half, bottle and all, in a cupboard, of which he always kept the key, and in the course of a couple of hours, he said to his assistant—

"Ben, could you catch a dog or a cat, do you think? Here is a little product from something I have, that I wish to try upon one."

"Yes, sir; I dare say I could." said Ben. "By-the-bye, Mrs. Griffiths, sir, has had a 'little cur given her by the hosier's wife opposite. I could get hold of that, sir, in half a minute, and it's an ill-tempered wretch."

"Get it, Ben—get it."

"I will, sir."

Ben left the laboratory, and presently returned with one of those fat fussy little dogs that look like a hearth-rug with an asthma, and which could hardly draw its breath, and from being pampered all its life with delicacies, had a bad digestion, which induced a bad temper, so that it was induced to snap at everybody that had the misfortune to come within its reach.

CHAPTER XVIII.

THE BREAKFAST AT BRUMMEL'S, AND THE VISIT OF CAPTAIN STRANGEWAYS.

BRUMMEL had said what was an arranged thing, when he told Captain Strangeways that he had to breakfast with the prince at two, on the morning following his mishap at Story's-gate by the Birdcage-walk, and accordingly a little after that hour, Sheridan and Master George duly arrived.

Sheridan had fully succeeded in quelling the suspicions of his illustrious companion, with respect to any share he might have been suspected to have had in the disappointment regarding Amelia Booker, and George entered so heartily into the fun of the trick that had been played upon Brummel, that he forgot everything else at the time, in his appreciation of it.

"You must not, of course, so much as hint at it," said Sheridan.

"Oh, there is no occasion; it is sure to come out."

"Yes, and with additions and corrections not by the author."

"Certainly, certainly—by-the-bye, what have you done about the green bottle, and the supposed poisonous contents?"

"Given both to Griffiths the chemist, who will come to us at the Mitre in Piccadilly to-night at ten, to let us know the result of an analysis he is going to make."

"Good, then come on to Brummel's at once, I long to hear what he has got to say; especially as you know exactly what did take place."

"Yes, I had it from the soldier. He wrote me a note; he must not suffer though."

"Oh no, I will see to that."

"Then I am satisfied, and here we are, so mum's the word."

"Ah, good morning," said Brummel, "good morning, be seated George, it's horridly early, ain't it?"

"No, I don't think it is very early for the time of year."

"Ah! ah! for what?"

"The time of year. Are you asleep yet?"

"Oh no, but you spoke of the time of the year, and upon my honour, I never know the time of year. There are lots of months, I believe, and some people always know their names, and so on, but, ah! ah! I never did."

"Ah! ah! ah!" laughed Sherry, "that's good. Now, if anybody had told that of you, Brummel, as an anecdote, people would have laughed, but doubted it for all that. But you look out of sorts a little, somehow—is that a bruise upon your hand?"

"Ah! ah! it may be. The fact is, I was in a little fracas in the park last night."

"Nothing uncivil I hope, that would be dreadful in the royal precincts too. I believe it's treason, is it not, George?"

"Why, yes, petty treason, I——"

"Very petty. You hear, Brummel, what George says, so you had better not be too free in your confessions."

"Oh, it's of no consequence—but the fact is—you don't eat—the fact is, I went to meet a genuine—thank you for the cream, Sherry—a feminine girl, ah, ah!"

"Indeed—and she came?"

"Of course."

Sherry kicked the prince, under the table.

"Of course she came, and yet as I was saying some tender nothings to her, there came up a fellow, a soldier of the Guards, and made a disturbance. Ah, ah, I was forced to cane the fellow. In the park, too—excuse me, George."

"Oh, don't mention it."

"I tell you what George shall do," said Sheridan, "as he is in a position no doubt to excuse, or cause to be excused, such a thing, he shall write a request to the effect that the caning in the park last night shall be looked over. You know a prosecution for brawling in the royal parks, Brummel, used to be punished by the loss of the right hand."

"Ah, yes, I was forced to cane the fellow."

"Captain Strangeways, sir," announced Brummel's valet.

"Who's that?" said the prince, while a slight frown contracted his eye-brows. "That's contrary to agreement, Brummel. What do you mean by keeping such lax discipline in your place as this? Get rid of your visitor."

"Gentlemen," said Strangeways, appearing at the door, "I hope I am not intruding upon you." The prince walked to the window, and looked out.

"Oh, my dear fellow," said Brummel to the captain, "George is particular, this is a sort of private meeting, you see, and I—I am much obliged—but of course you'll see that the soldier is properly punished—you understand. I caned *him*—do you understand that?"

"Oh, perfectly, sir, perfectly. I will not intrude upon your royal highness, but having been present last evening in the park, when Mr. Brummel had to cane a soldier, I merely called this morning to see how he was."

"Oh!" said the prince, turning from the window, "you were present?"

"I was, your highness."

"Then it is quite an understood thing amongst us, that the whole affair is to drop, as it might get Mr. Brummel into some trouble—you understand, sir. You will give my compliments to the colonel of the regiment, and say the affair is to drop."

"But is the fellow to be let off, sir?" said Captain Strangeways, with an appealing and puzzled look at Brummel.

"Let off," said Sheridan, "why, you say he has been caned, and I think it is Mr. Brummel who is being let off, and not the soldier whom you saw caned, as you say, sir."

Brummel bit his lip, and the gallant captain, seeing that things had taken an unlucky turn, made his bow, and backed out of the room as quietly as he could. But he got a look from Brummel, as he did so, which seemed to him translatable into "Let me see you again at some more fitting opportunity."

"Well, that's settled," said Sheridan; "and whom have we here?"

"Lord Chamois," said Brummel, "I think he was to come, you know."

"Oh! no objection to him. Ah, Chamois, how are you?" said the prince. "Why, you look frightfully dull to-day; what on earth is the matter with you, Chamois?"

"I look what I am," replied this nobleman, or rather son of a nobleman, for his title was only one of courtesy. "I look, then, just what I am, for I am as dull as—as Brummel's wit, or Sheridan's morality."

"And what about?"

"I don't mind telling you, because there's a sort of mystery about it, and that I can't exactly fathom yet, if ever I do."

"Hurrah! for a mystery," cried Sheridan. "Go on, while we eat and drink. I suppose some of your bony Scotch 'ancestors have been walking. Eh? Is that it? Or are your family and friends all convulsed by the apparition of a blade of grass growing actually upon your patrimonial flint fields?"

"No, you are wrong in both of your guesses, ingenious though they are."

"Then, for the love of lucidity, pray enlighten us."

"Listen; you know well that——"

"What's the use of telling us what we know well?"

"It's necessary for the elucidation of what is to follow. You know well that I am poor, and that I am waiting for a patrimony, which will not make me much the richer when I get it; but probably you have not been aware that I have for a considerable time been living upon promises."

"What does he mean?" said the prince.

"Promises to pay," added Chamois. "After mortgaging all the property of any sort or description that I had to mortgage, I was compelled to raise supplies of the needful by promissory-notes, at an exorbitant interest, which were all to be held off until I came into possession of the family acres, barren as you say they are, when one large mortgage was to settle all claims."

"Well," said Sheridan, "so long as a man can carry on the war, I don't think he ought to be over nice as to the how,"

"I have not been; but the affair that bothers me now is, that a Mr. Samuel Smith has sent me a letter——"

"And among all the Smiths," interrupted Sheridan, "you can't, for the life of you, find out which it is. I don't wonder at that bothering you or anybody."

"Wrong again. This Smith has a local habitation, as well as a name; but his letter is alarming—pray read it, Sherry, and tell me what you can make of it. I don't like the tone of it at all, I must confess."

He handed an open letter to Sheridan as he spoke, and it was read aloud as follows:—

"To Lord Chamois and Marchmont.   52, *Gray's Inn.*

"MY LORD,—A client of mine, having purchased of various people a number of bonds, judgments, promissory notes, mortgages, &c., &c., &c., all bearing your name, instructs me to proceed forthwith against you upon every one of them to the utmost extent of the law, unless, within seven days from the receipt of this, the before-mentioned bonds, judgments, bills, promissory-notes, &c., be not wholly and in full satisfied. My client's name is Mr. Samuel Smith, and many of the notes, bills, &c., are signed Marchmont. Your early reply will much oblige, my lord, your lordship's most obedient and humble servant,   JOHN BOYNE, Solicitor."

"Well," said Lord Chamois, "what do you think of that? It's rather too much for one day's work to think of paying up the liabilities of about eight years of London life."

"Rather; but it's of no consequence. It is only a draw, after all. You will find, of course, that this John Boyne has some proposal to make that will put money in his client's pocket, and leave you much as you were, with the exception that, when you have the means of so doing, you will be made to bleed a little more freely."

"You think so."

"Certainly I do, it needs no ghost to come to tell us that. I should advise that you give the man of law an interview, and ask him point blank what he has to propose; and when he finds that you understand him in that way, he will soon let you know how the affair stands."

"Well, I suppose it must be so; but it strikes me forcibly that when I do get the property, I shall have just to walk in and say, 'this is mine,' and then to turn round to my creditors, and say,—'Gentlemen, it is yours.'"

"Well, you cannot have your cake, and eat it likewise, you know."

"True, true—thank you for advice gratis."

"Which, I suppose, like most such, is not worth much. George, where are you off to?"

"I have an appointment at four, which I must keep. It is with a certain person, you know who."

"The deuce! About the two or three sixpences you are reported to owe, I suppose. Well, well, we live in a most rascally and unconfiding world; that's the fact. I think there ought to be, about once a year, a bill of indemnity passed, to all persons owing, or supposed to owe, anything up to a certain date. And then with what a pleasant freshness of feeling one could go on again—eh, George?"

"Remarkably so. Good morning,—I'm off."

"And I likewise. Good morning, Brummel, I think you have got out of your scrape in the park, do you know, remarkably well. You might have been heavily fined for brawling within the royal grounds, and your excuse that you went to meet a wench, I don't think, would have done you much good with certain royal personages I could mention."

"That it would not," said George, with a laugh.

"*Au revoir*," said Brummel, languidly.

In a few minutes the little party had left him, and then biting his lips, he muttered—

"I will have my revenge yet, though, against that soldier; and I rather think that I can convince Captain Strangeways it will be quite as well to modify the prince's message."

CHAPTER XIX.

LORD MARCHMONT HAS AN INTERVIEW WITH JOHN BOYNE IN GRAY'S-INN.

"PETER," said Mr. Boyne, the attorney, from his private room, at his chambers in Gray's Inn; "Peter."

"Yes, sir," said a half-starved-looking boy, appearing before his imperious master.

"I expect a gentleman to call here to-day who will give his name as Lord Chamois or Marchmont, for he is indiscriminately known as either; and when he does come, you will show him at once into my private room, and say I am not at home to anybody who calls while he is here."

"Yes, sir."

"And, Peter, by the bye, did you serve that writ last night upon Mr. Bulgin?"

"Oh, yes, sir, of course; I said I was a Mr. Thompson, and so saw him. He shook a little, sir."

"Very good. You will run to Chancery-lane, and tell Mr. Mobbles, the officer, that I shall want him to make the caption of Mr. Tremaine to-day. Ah! Tremaine came here yesterday and paid ten pounds on account, so it's quite time to take him, as he paid it to me only, without witnesses. I must get him to pay all expenses now, sink the ten pounds, and renew the whole debt for a month."

"Yes, sir."

"Be off with you. What's that to you, you scoundrel? How dare you stand loitering there, and listening to what don't concern you? I shall be the death of you some day. Peter, let me tell you a little anecdote, Peter. The last boy I had was transported."

"So I've heard, sir, for stealing a watch of yours, out of your private office, sir."

"You have heard right. But, Peter, come closer boy. He was innocent!"

"Innocent, sir!"

"Yes. What do you start at, fool? He knew too much, and he threatened, Peter, to tell something that he knew, so I thought it better to have him transported: ain't it a great moral warning to you, Peter, to keep your mouth always shut about my affairs?"

"Yes—yes—yes, sir."

"Go along with you, Peter?"

"But lord, sir, ain't you afraid to tell me such a thing?"

"Not at all, Peter: who do you suppose would believe such a grossly improbable thing, as that I should confide such a secret to you? I am quite safe, Peter, go along with you, and remember what I have said to you, go along."

Poor Peter did go along, looking about as scared at what his rascally master had said to him as that individual could possibly wish, and Mr. Boyne was perfectly safe in saying so much to poor Peter, for who would have for one moment believed the parish boy, if he said that the attorney had so committed himself to him? Oh, it was by far too improbable.

There are many Mr. Boynes in the world; people who have not come into contact with such specimens of the human race would scarcely believe it, but it is so for all that.

Peter had done all the out-of-door business that was required of him, and was cutting notches with an old penknife in the front of a desk, when there came a smart double rap at the door of the chambers, and the expected name of Lord Marchmont met the ears of Peter.

"Is Mr. Boyne at home?" asked the young nobleman, who, by-the-bye, was not so very young, for he would not see forty again.

"Yes, my lord. Please to walk this way," said Peter; and he duly announced the visitor to his master, who seemed to be so completely absorbed in the perusal of some contemplated deed as scarcely to notice the interruption. Peter closed the door.

"I beg your pardon, sir," said Boyne, with an assumed air of abstraction, "I beg your pardon, sir, but who did you say you were?"

"I am Lord Marchmont, and I came here on account of rather an extraordinary letter I received from you."

"Oh, yes, certainly, I recollect I had the honour of writing to your lordship. Ahem! Your lordship has come to settle, I suppose?"

"I have come for information."

"Of what description, may I ask, my lord?"

"Why I want to know who Mr. Smith is, and how it comes that I am indebted to him at all, for I don't know him."

"Mr. Smith, my lord, is a gentleman of large property, who has amused himself with buying up all your lordship's promissory obligations that were to be had in the market. I believe now he is nearly your lordship's only creditor. It's quite a legal speculation. The bills, notes, &c., have been all properly assigned, and he claims the gross sum of £35,162 10s. 4½d."

"Curse his fourpence-halfpenny!"

"Yes, my lord, putting out of the question the little expletive which your lordship has been pleased to use, that is Mr. Smith's claim. Oblige me by looking over that little account."

"This—why—why, it's a writ!"

"Exactly, my lord: I have the original here, if your lordship wishes to see it. It's just as well to serve you with it now, as to hunt after you all over the town, you see."

"I suspect you are a scoundrel, sir."

"Peter—Peter!"

"Yes, sir."

"Just prop the door open, and get your memorandum book ready. His lordship is kind enough to abuse me, and as some of it may be actionable, I wish you to be in a condition to swear to what his lordship may say. Now, my lord, say what you please."

"This is folly, Mr. Boyne; come to the point at once. What is it that is required of me now that I am here?"

"Peter!"

"Yes, sir."

"You can shut the door and put away your memorandum book. His lordship declines abusing for the present."

"I cannot waste the whole day with you, sir," added Lord Marchmont. "Tell me in plain language, what this Mr. Smith, who, I suppose, is just some gigantic usurer, requires of me, and you shall have as speedy an answer as I can possibly give to you upon the subject."

"Money, my lord, money. That's what Smith requires—money."

"How much? Money is a very indefinite expression, indeed; I want to know what the particulars of this plan of attack upon me happen to be, for that it is all duly arranged, I have no manner of doubt in the world."

"You are wrong then, sir,—my lord, I should say—you are wrong. There must be two parties to every agreement, and as in this case you must be one of them, and you have not yet come to any arrangement, it follows that it cannot all be so duly settled as your lordship supposes."

"I suppose, sir, I must wait your leisure. You know, and I dare say Mr. Smith, whoever he may be, knows likewise, that I cannot, at the present time, pay this money, or even any portion of it. I want to raise money, in point of fact, far from being able to pay any away."

"Oh! ah! hem!"

"What do you mean by that? There is something behindhand in all this, I am quite certain. I shall now, sir, bid you good day, and you can go on with your legal proceedings against me, or speak out in another shape, just as your leisure and your inclination may serve you."

"Stop, my lord. Let me tell your lordship what I, as an individual, think of this matter."

"Go on, sir; I will attend to you."

"I know Mr. Smith well. There is but one person in the world who has control over him, and that, I am sorry to say, is not myself, or you would not have been troubled in this manner. He will be inexorable. No doubt his object is to get possession of the whole of your estates. You will rot in prison, unless you consent to sacrifice everything you have in reversion or prospect. But—but—my lord, there is a person with whom you have influence, although you don't know it, who, in time, can throw all your bills, mortgage deeds, and notes into the fire, and so free you from the trammels of debt altogether, if she likes to do so."

"She—she? And who may she be?"

"Smith's daughter."

"The devil!"

"No, an accomplished, handsome woman, I assure you. When Smith made this dead set at you, as a mere matter of money, no doubt she protested against it. She had seen you—no matter when—and admired you. You are not so ugly as many people, I know."

"Thank you."

"And, in a word, fell in love with you. If you can return the lady's flame, you will be a free man, and have not a debt in the world. I know she could and would do that much with the old man, if she were sure of you for a husband."

"Husband? The devil!"

"I own the inconveniences of the situation. I am a husband of some experience, and my heart said Amen to your last pious remark on matrimony."

"And the lady has commissioned you to——"

"Hold, my lord; stop there. She has done no such thing; but I know something of human nature, and I am as well assured of what I say to you upon this subject, as if she had opened her mind to me completely upon it, which she most certainly has not."

"It's a strange affair."

"Well, it is rather so. But your lordship, with even your natural and acquired advantages, might do much worse than rid yourself of such heavy encumbrances, by a marriage with such a person as I have mentioned."

"Confusion take the whole affair. I must think—I must think. Yet no; what is the use of thinking? I cannot and will not sacrifice myself in this way. Let him do his worst."

"Very good, my lord. He will, and that will consist of an arrest directly. I have only thrown out a suggestion which, for the sake of all parties, I should have liked to see embraced before any suffering or inconvenience had ensued to your lordship. Already has Mr. Smith's daughter implored him not to take these steps against you; but all in vain—all in vain. Her loveliness—her tears were all in vain."

"Tears—loveliness!"

"Yes, my lord, she is lovely, and has a heart open as the day. Oh, if you knew her, you would love her."

"Perhaps not. Good morning, sir—I will think; and I suppose, at all events, I may rely upon nothing harsh being done until I have seen you again, sir."

"For three days, my lord."

"Three days only!"

"It is all, I dare say. For three days I will so procrastinate matters with Mr. Smith, that without his being able to charge me with neglecting his business, I shall still do nothing that shall incommode your lordship."

"Well, I suppose I ought to be obliged to you for that much latitude, and you can put it down in the bill, if it should come to a bill at all between you and I; so again, sir, I bid you a good day."

"Good day, my lord. Peter, Peter, show his lordship out directly. How inattentive you are, Peter!"

"Ha, ha!" laughed Mr. Boyne, when he was alone. "Booked, I should say—booked most decidedly. He has gone to think about it. Well, well—we shall see; he may, though, yet want a few days' lodging in a debtor's prison to bring him to a correct conclusion. Peter, you may go to your dinner—do you hear?"

"What a confounded scrape this is!" soliloquised Lord Marchmont. "Good God! the idea of marrying a money-lender's daughter. Oh, d—n it! no—I can't do it. The continent will do for me very well; I must be off to Holland. We are, thank God! at peace with somebody out of England. Yes, I will be off; and then, Mr. Smith, you may do your best, as well as your worst, for all I shall care."

CHAPTER XX.

THE SUPPER AT THE MITRE IN PICCADILLY, AND THE CHEMIST'S REPORT.

The Mitre tavern in Piccadilly was in its day a very noted place, and a very select place, too, or it would not have been honoured by the visits of the parties to whom we refer. It was to all appearance a private house, and no stranger would ever think of going to it, or if he had, he would not have been admitted except he came with a recommendation from some *habitue* of the place, or as an expected visitor to some party free of the premises.

There was one feature, too, in the mode in which the house was conducted, that at the first glance would not appear to be a very profitable one; and that was, that no money was taken of any of the visitors, that is to say, nothing was charged at the time, but every gentleman who was admitted as a guest was booked to the amount of his orders.

No doubt the proprietor of the Mitre lost a great deal of money by this sort of business, but no doubt he likewise gained a great deal, for unquestionably he got paid sometimes, and when that interesting operation did take place, his customers were not of a sort to look beyond the sum total of their account.

Very probably the bills of the Mitre were, by such worthies as those whom we have introduced to the reader, oftener paid than the more just and stringent claims.

But be that as it may, the party that assembled now in one of the most private and elegant rooms of that *recherche* establishment, certainly had no fear of what an amount they were running up against them in the books of the hotel, for they drank of the choicest wines that could be procured, and there was not a whim in the eating or drinking line that they did not carry out.

Sherry was eating a pine-apple, and pine-apples were then a guinea each, not being as now quite accessible to the million at the small charge of one-and-six.

"And so you really think now," said Colonel Hill, "that there will be found poison in the green bottle you brought from the widow's?"

"I do. But there is no occasion to call her a widow now, you know."

"True, true; poor unfortunate Booker has deprived her of that interesting appellation."

"He has. And I am willing to wager a dozen of the choicest vintage that can be procured by mine host of the Mitre here, that the report of our friend the chemist will be such as to confirm all the suspicions we can entertain upon the subject."

"We shall see," said George, "I understand you that you told him to come here at ten."

"I did, and the hour has nearly arrived. He will be punctual. He carries punctuality in every feature of his face. Are not these delicious olives?"

"Good enough. But you eat olives with pine apple, which is a most decided barbarism, as you, of all men, ought to be well aware. It's really too bad of you."

"Ha, ha! You don't know what you are talking about. But hold! Here comes James with some news. He looks like rumour full of tongues. Well, James, what is it?"

"A gentleman, sir, named Griffiths——"

"Admit him instantly. Now, my bloods, our chemist, our man of decoctions, unguents, and scruples, will tell us what he has discovered. Welcome, welcome—take a seat, Mr. Griffiths. I hope now, really, that you caught no cold last night."

The old chemist made a wry face, as with a rather impatient gesture he said—

"Let that pass. I have analyzed the contents of the green bottle, or rather half the contents, and I should wish that you would have the remainder analyzed by somebody else, so that there should be the confirmatory testimony of two chemists to the fact that it is a poison of a most terrific character."

"There," said Sheridan, as he struck his hand upon the table, "there, I told you so. Oh ye of little faith, did I not say as much from the first. Proceed, Mr. Griffiths, proceed."

"It is a poison that will not have an immediate or a startling effect upon the human frame, unless given in a large dose, but it is a poison which will insidiously and surely destroy life. That I have ascertained from actual experiment."

"The deuce you have. How is Mrs. Griffiths?"

"You mistake me," said the chemist; "I tried it upon a dog, not upon a—a—a——"

"Never mind what you were going to say," cried Mr. Sheridan; "we will each fill up the sentence, according to our several comprehensions of the case. The dog died?"

"Yes, but with no extraordinary symptoms. The creature died of debility—downright debility, I can assure you, and nothing else; and upon dissection nothing could be found to account for death, so that such a poison, in the hands of any one inclined to do mischief, would, indeed, be a frightful weapon."

"Take a glass of wine, Mr. Griffiths; we are much obliged to you—very much obliged to you. Perhaps you might be good enough to keep the poison by you until you hear further from me, about it. It was, and is at present, only a matter of curiosity, so that we will let it pass. By the bye, I have heard of poisons having as much effect, if they are introduced into the system through the blood as if taken in the stomach."

"More—more, as a general thing," said the chemist, "and I should say now that a very small portion of this poison, placed upon any spot where there had been an abrasion, so as to produce a wound, would very soon show its effects upon the system at large."

"It would?"

"Most certainly; a cut finger, for instance, would take it in, ay, or even a pin scratch might do so."

Sheridan glanced at his companions, as much as to say, "You hear what he says. Have you now any doubts regarding the guilt of Mrs. Mortimer?"

The conversation now evidently flagged a little, for the thoughts of all present had taken a mournful turn, and the old chemist fancied that it was more on account of his presence than anything else, that such a sudden cloud had come over any one's spirits, and he rose to go, saying as he did so—

"I shall keep the bottle and its contents carefully by me, then, since such is your wish, gentlemen, and I have the honour to wish you good night."

When he was gone, Sheridan rose, and in a voice of some excitement cried—

"Now for it. We know quite enough I should say, for our purpose, which is the purpose of justice. Is this Mrs. Mortimer to be allowed to go on in this career any longer—or are we to stop her at once, by giving such information as will cause her immediate apprehension?"

"We ought not to hesitate a moment," said the prince; "the police ought to see to the affair though, not we, for after all you know that, as the evidence against her principally rests upon Sherry's dream, I don't think much can be done against her. Suppose we go off at once to the Wheatsheaf, and see how she seems."

"Agreed—agreed," cried all, and in a few moments the party at the Mitre was broken up, and was making its way towards Pimlico, where dwelt the now most undoubtedly guilty Mrs. Booker. We shall step a little before them, and see what is doing at the tavern.

There was a kind of strange fluttering uneasiness about Mrs. Booker when Sheridan left the house, on that evening of the supper, to which he had so audaciously invited himself, which she could not very well define; but which, the more she tried to combat with, only came upon her with greater force and vehemence.

Her colour went and came occasionally, like the fitful hues of an April day, and she now and then glanced at Mr. Booker, with an expression on her countenance of so much painful interest, that any one would have thought her the most affectionate of wives, and that she so bitterly bemoaned the cut finger as to make herself quite unhappy about the surely trivial enough accident.

Mr. Thompson's spirits visibly declined when Mr. Sheridan was gone, and he soon himself took his departure, after shaking his old friend, Booker, most heartily by the hand, and likewise

bestowing the same pledge of friendship upon his wife, which was more than he had thought to have done when he first came to the house. But then Mrs. Booker had, as she generally did, succeeded in throwing some of the spell of her fascinations around Mr. Thompson.

It was quite late enough to think of retiring to rest; but Mr. Booker went first, leaving his wife alone for a time in the bar parlour.

It was strange that, notwithstanding her uneasiness, and that sensation of something wrong which had beset her all the evening, it never struck her for a moment as desirable to see that the little green bottle was safe, and yet a remarkably clever woman was Mrs. Booker,

No. 8.

and one would really have thought that nothing of a probable character would have escaped her penetration. But so it was—the circumstance did escape it.

We see in the every-day cases of criminality that are brought before our courts most wonderful instances of a kind of infatuation in persons who have committed great crimes, who, after arranging everything with the most consummate tact, as they fully believe, leave some point unguarded, which is evident to the meanest observer.

Thus the assassin will ram down the powder and ball in his gun with a paper that shall be damning evidence against him. The thief will carry about in his pocket some valuable trinket until he is captured, and that shall be the means of convicting him of his robbery.

But such things are of such daily occurrence that one ceases to wonder at them, but receives them as part and parcel of the ordinary phenomena of human intellect.

And thus we may for a brief moment or two wonder that Mrs. Booker never thought of looking to the safety of her little green bottle in the bureau, and then we must just content ourselves with the fact that she did not think of the possibility or the probability of its abstraction.

Well, then, when Mr. Booker was gone to bed, she sat with her head resting upon her hands, for some time, and leaning upon the table, while by the tremulous motion of her fingers, and the deep moans that occasionally came from her heart, it seemed that she was in great mental agony.

At length she spoke.

"Yes," she said, "the day and the hour have now nearly come. What I have been striving for for twelve years has come at last, and I shall have my revenge. Like a personification of destiny I shall swoop upon my victim—I, who was his victim. The time has come—the time has come; but oh, what have I not waded through to the attainment of this object?"

For a time she was silent again, and once or twice something like a sob seemed to come from her lips, and then she rose to her feet, and dashed aside some scalding tears from her eyes, as she said—

"How is it that this most unwonted mood has come over me now, when most I have need of all the firmness I can call to my aid? It must not, it shall not be said that I faltered at the last—I, who have lived to prove, or nearly so, the axiom that there is a way to the accomplishment of any mortal object, if they who pant for it have but courage enough to tread the course."

She stole softly up to the bed-room. Mr. Booker had retired to rest, and was sleeping; but as she stood on tiptoe and listened, she fancied that his breathing was irregular and disturbed.

"So soon," she muttered "so soon. Well—well, 'tis better that it should be so—'tis much better—it is all over now—at least the worst is over, and to-morrow I commence a new career."

She looked at herself in the dressing-glass, and she shuddered as she did so, for never had she seen herself so ghastly pale before.

"This will not do," she muttered. "Am I, at the eleventh hour, to mar all from a foolish nervousness? Oh no—no—I will and must be firm—firm as a rock; and when my tale is told to gaping listeners, in after years, it shall not be said that Widow Mortimer went so far, and then paused, through terror, of not what she had to do, but of what she had done. What —what is that?"

She fancied she had heard a sound of alarm in the room, and she almost fainted from excess of terror. It was nothing but one of those accidental slight noises made by pieces of furniture at times; but most truly might she have said, "Conscience doth make cowards of us all."

CHAPTER XXI.

THE ASTOUNDING ANNOUNCEMENT TO MR. BOOKER, WHO IS ASKED TO PLAY A DIFFCULT
PART.

As the party from the hotel in Piccadilly proceeded rather noisily towards the Widow Mortimer's at Pimlico (we cannot help calling her at times the Widow Mortimer—it seems her most natural name), the members of it began to get serious, and finally they paused, just by the corner of Hyde Park, where the much maligned Wellington statue now awaits its doom, to hold a consultation.

"You know, all of you," said Colonel Hill, "that this is really rather a serious affair, and it strikes me as a foolish thing for us to go where we are now going, without some definite plan of action."

"True enough," said Sheridan. "I have been thinking the same thing for the last five minutes. Here we are, all of us, *en route* to Mrs. Booker's, without knowing what we mean to do when we get there."

"But it's at your suggestion," said George, "that we are so *en route*."

"Right again. But second thoughts are best, you know, in many cases, although not in shooting pheasants, so I say, let us consider. Now, what say you to my going alone, and, as before, getting a bed for the night in the house, and so taking accurate observations of what Mrs. Booker is about?"

"Be it so," said the prince, who, from the first, had not seemed to relish the adventure, or to like the idea of going to the tavern. "You can tell us all about it, Sherry, you know, to-morrow night."

"Agreed—I will. And now I will set all my wits to work to arrive at the real truth, as regards the intention of Mrs. Booker; for, after all, we don't know that she knows the contents of the green bottle to be poison. I will own, I am quite ready to admit that all the circumstantial evidence is against her, and I will own that I have no doubt sufficiently strong to make a point of, but yet there is a bare possibility the other way."

"But what will you do?" said Hill.

"That shall entirely depend upon circumstances. I think, though, at present, that it would be very wrong not to warn Booker of his situation, and, at all events, let him know what has happened. You know I have an ally, too, in the house, in the shape of Miss Amelia."

"Yes," said George; but somehow you never exactly explained to us how it was you all of a sudden made such great friends with that young lady."

"No—nor do I mean. That's my secret, but it may come out some day, although at present, as the newspapers say when they have killed somebody—who writes to say he is alive and kicking—the news is 'premature.'"

Waving his hand, then, to his friends, by way of adieu for the night, Sheridan went on alone to the tavern, where he hoped to be able to accomplish something for the deliverance of poor Booker from the really very critical position he was then in; for if Mrs. Booker found she was thwarted one way, there was no knowing exactly, she being a strong-minded woman, what new course she might adopt for the accomplishment of the objects she sought from Booker's decease.

"Yes," thought Sherry to himself as he neared the tavern, "knowing what I do, I have no sort of right in the world to keep poor Booker in such a perilous state. But first I will hold a consultation, if I can, with Amelia."

The hour was not quite such an unseasonable one, as many at which the doors of the taverns were opened to admit known visitors, so that he found no difficulty in procuring admission. Mrs. Booker, herself, was not visible, but Mr. Booker was in the bar-parlour, a very unusual thing for him at that time of night.

He knew Sheridan when he came in, and in reply to an interrogatory as to how he was, he shook his head in a very dubious manner, as he was about to make some complaint, and then, as if suddenly thinking better of it, he said quickly—

"Oh, very well—very well indeed, sir."

"But how is it you are up so late? I only came for a bed."

"Why, sir, the fact is, Mrs. B. has gone out, and I am waiting for her to return."

"Oh, indeed; and is your niece at home?"

"Oh, yes; gone to bed."

"What an opportunity," thought Sheridan, "for a confidential chat with Booker;" and then, thinking, probably, that he should never have a better opportunity of saying what he had to say, he told Maria that he would not keep her up, but that if she told him the number of his room, and left him a chamber candlestick, all would be right, as he would sit a little while with Mr. Booker. He drew his chair closer to that gentleman, and said—

"Mr. Booker, are you a happy man?"

Booker gave a groan.

"Ah, I understand you."

"Why, Mr. Sheridan," said Booker, "the truth is, that my wife is a fine woman, and sooth to say, an educated woman, and in her way, not altogether an unamiable woman; but since I have heard about my being her seventh husband, I certainly have hardly known a moment's peace, and I find myself continually saying, 'what's become of the other six?'"

"No doubt. An exceedingly natural question. And what does she say to that?"

"She—she! What Mrs. B.?"

"Yes, to be sure. Who else?"

"Why, you don't fancy I say it to her, do you, surely?"

"Yes, to be sure, Booker; to whom else could you say it with so much propriety? I think that, situated as you are, it is an extremely pertinent question."

"Oh no, I could not say it to her; it's to myself, sir, I am always saying it. Perhaps I say it in my sleep, and then she may hear it, and I often think I must have done so, for this morning she looked, very odd at me, and said, while she was dressing, "How do you feel yourself this morning, Mr. B——? Have you any headache at all ?"

"Oh, and what did you say ?"

" 'No,' said I, 'no, what makes you ask ?' 'Oh,' says she, 'nothing particular, only you have passed a disturbed night, rather, and that made me a little anxious. Do you know, I think she is a little anxious about me, sir."

"Mr. Booker, this is an apportunity of speaking to you, which I hardly expected, but which —what's that ?"

"What's what, sir ?"

"I heard a noise, like a key turning in the lock, and a door shutting."

"Perhaps it's Mrs. B—— come home; she has a latch-key, and always let's herself in; I'll go and see. How very provoking if it be, for you were going to tell me something, I am sure, that would have been very interesting."

"Most provoking," said Sheridan; "go and see at once, will you, Mr. Booker, and if it be your wife, I will go to my bed-room at once, of course."

"Mr. Booker returned in a few moments to say that it was a false alarm, for that the street door was close shut, and no one was there at all.

"Well, then," added Sheridan, "I have that to tell you which will cause you both surprise and indignation. You have asked often, you say, the question of, where are the six husbands of Mrs. Booker? and what I have now to detail to you will have the effect, I think, of enabling you to append the answer to the inquiry."

Mr. Booker looked alarmed, but what were his first looks to those that gradually crept over his face as Sheridan told him the full particulars of all that occurred.

The pipe he had been smoking dropped from his hand; his eyes looked as fixed and unspeculative as those of a dead mackerel; and finally, with a groan, he slipped off his chair, and sat upon the floor, looking the picture of horror and dismay.

"Rouse yourself, Mr. Booker, rouse yourself," said Sheridan, "I had no idea my communication would have had this effect upon you, or you should not have had it from me so abruptly."

"Oh, oh, oh, oh!" said Booker.

"Why, what's the use of sitting there, and saying oh ? That will not mend the matter; you are not hurt, and you ought, at all events, to rejoice that you have escaped."

"Oh, oh, oh, oh !"

"Confound the fellow, I can make nothing of him. Mr. Booker, do you hear me or do you not ?"

"Oh, oh, oh, oh !"

"What a perplexing thing, to be sure. Oh, indeed! And yet perhaps I may restore him by any sudden excitement. Let me see; perhaps, this may suffice; I can but try."

He took from his pocket an elegant gold snuff-box, and taking out a massive pinch, he placed it on the lid, and then holding it close to Mr. Booker's nose, he with one puff of his breath, blew it at him. A general contortion of countenance, and then a loud sneeze proclaimed the effect.

"How are you now ?"

"Bet-bet-better a—a—a—I—I—oh!"

"That will do: don't sneeze for a month, that's a good fellow, but get up and sit down, and talk to me rationally, if you can, about what I have just now communicated to you, for you know it concerns you very nearly indeed."

Mr. Booker was much revived by the snuff, but he was still in a terrible fright, although he did manage, with a little assistance, to seat himself upon his chair, instead of upon the floor; and then he looked at Sheridan with such a lugubrious expression of face, that it was enough to make anybody laugh, and grave as were the circumstances of the case, Sheridan could not for the life of him, refrain from smiling.

"Why, you are not hurt, Booker," he said.

"Oh, ah, not hurt!" said Booker, who seemed to have become almost idiotic all of a sudden, for he looked at himself all down, beginning at one of the buttons of his waistcoat and only ending at his toes, "Oh, ah, not hurt! Oh, dear no, who said I was ?"

"Botheration," muttered Sheridan, "this was an error of judgment, telling this man anything about it. Booker, here is your brandy-and-water; perhaps you will be better if you drink this."

"Oh, ah!" said Booker, in an abstracted way, "perhaps I shall be better if I drink that. Oh, yes, anything else. What's become of the other six, eh, eh?"

He mechanically drank up the brandy-and-water, and then Sheridan tried him again by saying—

"Now, Booker, you of course are the proper person to take some steps in the business; do you understand what I say?"

"Oh, ah, perhaps he'll be better if he drinks his brandy-and-water," said Booker.

"It's of no use—it's of no use, Mr. Booker; what the devil do you mean to do? Are you going to remain here, or are you going to leave? You have parted already with your wits. How could I be so foolish as to make such a communication to such a man?"

"Perhaps," said Booker, still speaking in the same strange, abstracted tone, "perhaps he will be better if he takes his brandy-and-water. Oh, ah—yes. Oh, yes."

"Well, this is provoking, to be sure. He will spoil everything. But justice must not be thwarted and circumvented because Mr. Booker has taken leave of his senses. I must think of some other course, and that immediately too. And this demoniacal woman—this widow—"

"Well, sir," said Mrs. Booker, suddenly opening the door a short distance only, and just showing herself upon the threshold; "well, sir, what of this widow?"

"Murderess!" cried Sheridan, and he sprang to his feet; "murderess! you shall not escape. You have no doubt been listening, and have heard all."

"I have," said Mrs. Booker, and as she uttered the words, she slammed the door of the bar parlour close, and locked it in a moment on the outside, so that Sheridan and Mr. Booker, the latter of whom had again slid off his chair and sat down upon the floor when he saw his wife, were prisoners.

Then there was a hurried footstep in the passage. The street door was opened, and then shut again with a bang that shook every window in the house, and was enough to alarm the whole street. Mrs. Booker had made her escape even at that critical moment.

CHAPTER XXII.

A GENERAL ALARM, AND THE MYSTERIOUS APPEARANCE OF TATTAM THE DRUMMER.

PERHAPS a remarkably skilful hand at the enumeration of figures might have counted twenty before Sheridan recovered from the astonishment into which he was thrown by the audacious appearance and disappearance of Mrs. Booker. Then he made a rush at the door, but it was but to be confirmed in the idea that the crunching noise like the extraction of a large tooth from the head of a giant, which he had just heard, was the locking of the door by Mrs. B.

"A prisoner!" he exclaimed.

"Oh, oh, oh!" said Booker. "Per'aps he will be better if he takes his brandy-and-water."

The door was not a remarkably strong one, but unfortunately it opened inwards to the room, so that there was a great disadvantage in trying to force it from the room. Probably from the passage that object might have been easily enough accomplished, as there would have been nothing but the lock to contend against. As it was, however, Sherry soon made the discovery that his strength was insufficient to force the door open, and when he was assured of that fact, he began ringing the bell so loudly that he soon alarmed the house.

Maria came forth to the scene of action.

"Help! help!" cried Sherry, from within; "the door's locked. Open it, Maria, at once, and let me out."

Maria did so, and there was quite a little struggle in the doorway, between her and Sheridan, to see whether she should get in first, or he should get out, and when she saw Mr. Booker seated on the floor, looking to all appearance like a man in some very desperate state indeed, she thought that some fearful accident had taken place, and raised a loud cry of dismay.

"Where's your mistress—where's Mrs. Booker?" said Sheridan, as he placed his back against the street door, with a vague but not very strong notion that she might be in the house, "Where is Mrs. Booker?"

"Not come home yet," said Maria. "But what has happened to Mr. Booker. Oh, sir, are you dead?"

"Perhaps he will be better after his brandy-and-water," said Booker. That was his mania.

"Your mistress has a key," said Sherry, "I suppose, and lets herself in."

"Oh, yes; a key of the patent lock that's on the street door. She always lets herself in quite quietly."

"And out, too," added Sherry. "By Heaven she has made her escape!"

"Escape, sir!"

"Don't ask me any questions, whatever you do. Oh, Amelia, have you heard the alarm?"

"I have," said Amelia, who made her appearance at that moment, rather hastily dressed.

"What has happened? I was afraid at first that the tavern was on fire."

"Worse—worse, Amelia."

"Worse than that. What is it? oh, what is it? How is my poor uncle? Where is he?"

"Hush! Don't be alarmed. Come with me into the bar-parlour, and I will tell you all about it."

Amelia followed him with looks of alarm, and then he told her all that had occurred, concluding by saying—

"Of course your aunt must have come in while I was speaking to your uncle; and, unfortunately for the cause of truth and justice, she overheard me make to him a revelation which so much concerned her safety. Indeed there was a noise which ought to have put me more upon my guard. But the end of it all is, that she now has a full knowledge of all that can be said against her, and that she has escaped."

"Oh, wretched, unhappy woman," said Amelia.

"You pity her?"

"Indeed I do. Can you imagine, sir, any class of society more entitled to our pity than the guilty?"

"That is true enough, for they must sooner or later be the most wretched. Now, however, Amelia, to leave out of the question all philosophy—what shall be done?"

"I know not; I feel half distracted at the suddenness of the affair. Must it be made public?"

"Most unquestionably it must now."

"And my poor uncle?"

"Oh, he will recover, I dare say. He seems to have received a terrible mental shock by what I told him; indeed, I could have hardly thought it possible he should have been so deeply affected. Only look at him now, Amelia."

There sat Mr. Booker, on the floor, with the same vacant look, and Amelia spoke kindly to him, saying—

"Uncle, dear uncle, pray rise. There is no danger. Get up, uncle, and behave yourself differently. It is you who ought to direct what is to be done in this most mysterious and unhappy piece of business."

"Perhaps he will be better after his brandy-and-water," said Booker.

"There, Amelia," remarked Sherry, "nothing can be got out of him but those words. They and they only seem to have taken a firm hold of his imagination. Probably rest will do him good, and after a sound sleep he may awaken, quite able to cope with the circumstance. As for me, it now becomes my positive duty to go to a magistrate, and tell him all that I know; it would be criminal in me to neglect doing so for any length of time now."

"It must be so," replied Amelia, "I can understand well that it must be so. Will you however, sir, before you leave the house, see my uncle to his room?"

"Oh, yes, with pleasure."

Tom, the pot-boy, was roused up from somewhere in the lower regions, where he slept, and in which peaceful retreat he had heard nothing of the disturbances that had alarmed everybody else in the place; and between him and Sherry, the nearly helpless Mr. Booker was conveyed up stairs to his room.

There was the bed, in which he had laid down innocently to sleep by the side of her whose conscience must surely at times have been afflicted with the remembrance of her crimes; and there, upon the toilette table, were various little elegancies, which Mrs. Booker liked to have about her. It was quite evident, from the state of the apartment, that when she had gone out, she had by no means calculated upon not returning to it again. Some jewels were lying upon the dressing-table, and likewise a small purse with some money in it, but not to a large amount.

"Lor, sir," said Tom, the pot-boy, "what *upses* and *downses* there is in this here world, ain't there?"

"Certainly there are."

"Now, sir, who'd a thought that my missus would a turned out anything wrong, a'ter all. The idea now, sir, o' poor master taking on in this here sort of way, too. Come, master, hold up, while I gets off this here boot. There you is now; sir, just give him a hoist along o' me, and he'll be in bed in a minute, sir, that he will, and as snug as nothing."

The hoist was given to Mr. Booker, and no doubt he would have been snug enough if the fates had not had another rather remarkable surprise in store for him."

Amelia had lighted Sherry and Tom, as they conveyed Mr. Booker to his bed-room, and then she had placed the candle upon the dressing-table and gone away, while Tom went through the process of unrobing his master. The bed—a large old-fashioned one, with massive hangings, was at the further end of the room, so that it was greatly in the shade, but yet sufficiently visible not to render it necessary to carry the candle to it for the purpose of putting Mr. Booker into it.

What was their surprise, however, not unmingled with some amount of consternation, to hear a loud cry of murder, the moment they threw him on to the bed, and then a voice added—

"Oh, don't. What's that?—oh, murder! murder! The house is tumbling down!—oh—oh —murder!"

"The devil!" said Sheridan, as he ran to the toilette table for the light.

"Is it the devil, sir?" said Tom, and then without waiting for an answer to his question, he took to his heels, leaving his coadjutor to reap whatever glory or danger there might be to be earned in the bed room which contained so unquestionable a customer.

Sheridan was not, like the Athenians, given to superstition, so he at once got the light and darted back to the bed again, when certainly, a very strange and unexpected sight presented itself.

Sitting up in bed, and holding Mr. Booker fiercely by the collar, while the latter lay help-lessly muttering still about the brandy-and-water, was a boy in the full dress of a drummer in the Guards, upon whose face fear was struggling with resentment.

For a few moments, such was the surprise of Sheridan at this most unexpected apparition, that he continued holding the candle at arm's length, and staring at it without speaking. He could hardly believe himself awake. At length he found breath to say—

"Who in the name of all that's wonderful are you?"

"Joe Tattam, the drummer, sir—oh, have mercy upon me!"

"Mercy upon you. What on earth do you mean? How came you here, you scoundrel?"

"Yes, sir, I begs your pardon—that's just it, sir. How came I here—you see, sir, I thought I was doing it uncommonly snug—I did, sir, and so I fell asleep."

"That is no explanation—I shall hand you over to a constable."

"No, don't do that, sir, I shall get into trouble," said the drummer, as he got off the bed— If you will promise, sir, not to say anything about it, I will tell you all."

"Go on, then."

"You promise me, sir, that you won't tell anybody, because if you did, it might get the young lady into trouble."

"Young lady—what young lady?"

"Miss Amelia Booker—it was she as I came to see."

"The deuce you did—why, you infernal scoundrel, you don't mean to tell me that you came here as a visitor to that young lady; I will not believe one word of it. This is merely an excuse—you meant to rob the house."

"Not I, sir—we of the Guards never do such things—do you know Tom Atterbury, sir?"

"A soldier."

"Yes, in my regiment, and it was on his account I came to bring a letter to Miss Amelia. He told me there was an individual in the shape of an aunt, that I must avoid, so I thought to do the thing cleverly; and after getting some beer down stairs, I took an opportunity when nobody was looking and popped up here. The fact is, you see, sir, I wanted to find out which was the young lady's bed-room."

"You scoundrel—well, well, go on—what next?"

"Why, sir, somehow or another, I got into this room, and then, hearing a noise of somebody coming, I popped into the bed to be out of the way."

"When was that?"

"About half an hour ago, sir."

"Well, what then—did anybody come into the room?"

"Oh, yes, sir; a stoutish, good-looking woman came in, and a deuce of a hurry she did seem to be in, to be sure. She turned out several boxes and took away a lot of papers with her, and as she left the room, I heard her say just the two words—'For ever.'"

"And what then?"

"Oh, why then, sir, it seems I fell asleep, for I don't recollect anything else quite clear about it, till somebody—your friend there, who keeps saying something about brandy-and-water—came bounce on top of me, and nearly crushed me flat. You ought to have considered, old chap, you ain't one of the lightest weights in the world, you know."

"If your story be true," said Sheridan, "you have the letter to Amelia Booker?"

"And here it is, sir."

The drummer, as he spoke, produced a sealed note, and then Sheridan took him down stairs, leaving Mr. Booker to repose, and sending Maria for Amelia, he told her the adventure with Joe Tattam the drummer, and handed her the note, which when she opened, she found contained the following words :—

"AMELIA,—Before I undergo the disgrace of a military punishment, I wish to bid you a last farewell, which I do now in these few words. I know not whether you really have any affection for me or not, but if you have any lingering feeling of kindness for your unhappy Atterbury, chase it from your heart, and cease to remember one who, in a short time, will be a corpse, for I will not live after enduring the punishment to which they have so unjustly condemned me. Farewell, dear—dear Amelia, for ever !"

The colour forsook the cheeks of Amelia as she read the epistle, and when it was concluded, she looked as if she was very much inclined to faint.

CHAPTER XXIII.

LORD MARCHMONT MAKES UP HIS MIND TO CHOOSE THE LEAST OF TWO EVILS.

LORD MARCHMONT did not by any means feel particularly happy at the prospect before him. The delightful choice of rotting in a debtor's prison, as Mr. Boyne, the attorney, called it so graphically, or of marrying the daughter of the mysterious Mr. Smith, did not, to his mind, present itself in lively and attractive colours.

He could not say with Macheath—"How happy could I be with either," for either was an alternative of a most blood-curdling character to him.

He was very peculiarly situated. The principal expectations he had in after life consisted in his keeping some portions of his family ignorant of the damning amount of his debts and liabilities; and if the Mr. Smith, who had so vexatiously and unaccountably taken a fancy to buy up all such debts and liabilities, chose to do so, he certainly might make the fact of his, Lord Marchmont's, pecuniary involvements sufficiently notorious.

He took the advice of some friends.

Now friends always advise, if they advise at all sincerely, something that is much more to our interest than it is consonant to our feelings, and Lord Marchmont found that there was but one opinion prevalent, and that was, that he should get rid of his debts in exchange for— Miss Smith, if that was her name.

In vain he twisted and turned the affair over in his mind, in every possible shape and way. There was nothing to be done with it but that he must consent to the marriage ; but he made up his mind that he would take good care not to be saddled with both the wife and the debts.

"No—no," he said. "I will not be taken in that way, at all events. When I give my hand to the lady, the bonds and bills must be returned to me. That must be a clear understanding with old Smith—the scoundrel. I wonder what sort of a looking animal it is."

Such were the reflections of his lordship as, within the appointed time of grace from further process, he made his way to Gray's Inn, and once again tapped at the door of Mr. Boyne's chambers.

Peter, as usual, answered the summons, but there was now some one with the attorney, and therefore his lordship had to sit down for a time in Peter's room.

This outer office was not a very choice specimen of domestic architecture. The fact is, that the inside, or better rooms of chambers in many of the inns of courts, are not very luxurious abodes ; and, it is a matter of absolute necessity that the outer room, in which the clerk luxuriates, should be not so good as the master's apartment, it is, on the principle of all high-flying radical levelling, left alone, while the room that should be better is dragged down to its uncomfortable level.

In a little dirty hole, then, about eight feet square, sat poor Peter.

For about five minutes there was a silence as of the grave between his lordship and Peter, after which, Peter wrote something on a small slip of paper, and handed it over to Lord Marchmont, who thereupon read—

"Mr. Smith is with him."

"Oh," said Marchmont, " do you mean the Mr. Smith who has interested himself so much in my affairs."

"Hush! I do. Don't speak above your breath, if you must speak, and every now and then say something about the weather, in case he should be listening to you."

"I will. It's tolerably fine walking. Who the deuce is this Mr. Smith?"

"I dare say it is. I don't exactly know; but you have only got to hold out, and then they will come to terms. I can tell you that to a certainty, and what's more, I rather suspect that between you and this Mr. Smith, is a——"

Tingle, tingle went Mr. Boyne's bell, and Peter jumped up, and went to the inner room to answer the summons.

In about half a minute he emerged, showing out a man, who was so completely wrapped up in a cloak trimmed with fur, that nothing of him could be seen but the cloak, his boots, and his hat, together with the smallest possible bit of his face.

Lord Marchmont, after the piece of information he had received respecting the identity of this personage with the Mr. Smith who held his fortunes in his hands, looked at him, as may well be supposed, with some degree of curiosity and attention; but, before he could make up his mind to speak to him, he was gone.

"Pray walk in, my lord," said Mr. Boyne.

No. 9.

Lord Marchmont followed him into his inner room, and, when the door was shut, the lawyer very civilly indeed handed him a chair, and then was silent.

"I have come to you again," said Marchmont, "according to promise, and I must say that I am repugnant to what you propose to me. It is scarcely to be considered likely that I should make so great a sacrifice, sir."

"Very well, my lord, I hope your lordship has duly considered all the consequences attendant upon your lordship's decision."

"Of course, sir, I quite understand, from the little document, in the shape of a writ, which you were so kind as to hand to me upon the occasion of my last visit here, that Mr. Smith has commenced legal proceedings."

"Your lordship's estimate of that little circumstance is uncommonly correct, I can assure you. But you are well aware, that in the number of bonds, judgments, bills, &c., which are now in the possession of Mr. Smith, and all bearing your name—there are many upon which he can arrest you at once."

"Well, sir."

"And others, upon which he would elect, as a matter of right to you, that there should be lawsuits concerning."

"Well, sir."

"Then, my lord, since you have made your election to abide by the consequences of refusing the little family arrangemnt, which Mr. Smith, I think, would come into, and which his daughter would most certainly accede to, from genuine good feeling and affection towards your lordship, the result will be, that your lordship, if your lordship has not already dined, will dine in the Fleet-prison."

"So soon."

"Yes, my lord, you will find that this is an office in which unnecessary delays are not at all encouraged."

"Perhaps, Mr. Boyne," said his lordship, and he spoke with more asperity, than he had yet shown during the whole affair, "perhaps, Mr. Boyne, you might find my caption not quite so easy and straightforward as you seem to imagine."

"I must confess, my lord, that I don't see the difficulty."

"Indeed. And pray how would you set about it, then—since you are so frank and candid in this business?"

"Really, I should open that window just behind your lordship, and which looks into South-square, in the inn, and beckon to the sheriff's-officer, who is waiting upon the steps opposite, and then he would come up and take your lordship as easily as possible, to my apprehension."

"So! I am trapped that way, am I?"

"Trapped, my lord—that is a very ungracious word, and I am not quite sure but it is actionable; however, we will, if your lordship pleases, say no more about that just now, and I will open the window, and call in our friend opposite, which will put an end to what, with your lordship's determination as to your course of proceeding, cannot be but an unprofitable interview to both of us.'

"Stop," said Lord Marchmont, after he had gone to the window, and, by looking opposite, actually satisfied himself that there was a suspicious-looking man sitting on the opposite door steps. cracking nuts.

"At your lordship's service."

"What security have I, that by agreeing to the extraordinary proposition of marrying the lady you mention, I shall accomplish my object, as regards freeing myself from debt?"

"Your lordship shall have placed in your own hands, ten minutes before the ceremony commences, every bill and bond to which your name is attached."

Still, for a few moments he hesitated, during which time, Mr. Boyne very elaborately mended a pen. It was true that Lord Marchmont had all but made up his mind before he went to Gray's Inn, to accept of the conditions named; but he shrunk, when it actually came to the point for him to do so. Speak, however, he must, and during those few moments of painful and agitating thought, the image of one whom he really loved, and with whom he would have been but too happy to have contracted a union, rose up before him, like a reproaching spirit.

He sighed deeply, and with a smart crack, Mr. Boyne nibbed the pen.

"Well, sir," he said, at length, "I am a man, I suppose——"

"I suppose you are, my lord."

"Do not interrupt me, sir, I was about to say, that I am a man who must yield to destiny."

"I beg your lordship's pardon, you certainly are."

"I, however, should like an interview with the lady before I irrevocably pledge my honour to the match."

"Oh, my lord, the lady would not take your lordship's honour."

" Sir."

"I only speak according to my instructions—if you say to me now that you consent, subject to the return, ten minutes before the ceremony takes place, of all your bonds and bills, and if you mean to do what you say, you can have no objection to write as much."

"No—no. I will not give a written promise of marriage."

"Very good, my lord. Don't disturb yourself. Just allow me to open that window. Oh, I perceive my friend with the nuts is still there. Hey! hey! hey!"

Lord Marchmont sat looking very sullen, and there was in a few minutes a heavy tramp upon the stairs. Mr. Boyne slid a paper before him, on which, in plain round text, was written the following, to him most harrowing words—

"I hereby promise to marry the only daughter of Mr. Samuel Smith, named Jane, provided that, ten minutes before the performance of the ceremony, she, or some other person on her behalf, hands to me all my bonds, bills, judgments, mortgage deeds, promissory notes, &c. &c., given by me to any and all persons whatsoever, on account of monies owing by me, for and on any account whatsoever, that she may be possessed of."

"Is that Mr. Bugsby, the bailiff, Peter?"

"Yes, sir."

" Just tell him to walk this way, Peter, if you please, and don't be all day about it. Now, my lord, if you please?"

Lord Marchmont read the document again. The bailiff's tread was heard plainly in the outer room. His lordship knew from a day and a night's former experience what a debtor's prison was, and he shuddered.

Mr. Boyne slowly moved the inkstand towards him. For about the space of time that any one might have counted five, they looked at each other in silence. Then, with a desperate kind of eagerness, Lord Marchmont seized one of the pens and scrawled his signature at the foot of the paper.

"It's done," he said.

"Yes," added the lawyer, as he put his own name to it as a witness. "I rather think it is. Peter! Peter!"

" Yes, sir."

" You need not trouble Mr. Bugsby, the Sheriff's officer, to come into this room. You can tell him he will be paid his caption fee, Peter, but his lordship and I have succeeded in settling affairs amicably without him. Do you understand, Peter?"

" Yes, sir."

CHAPTER XXIV.

THE DANGEROUS SITUATION OF TOM ATTERBURY.—THE PRINCE ACTS PRINCELY.

Lord Marchmont has taken such a decided step in life, that we may very well leave him for the present, to think of it and its consequences, while we go back to the tavern, where we left poor Amelia, so much affected at the letter of her soldier lover, Tom Atterbury.

"Ah, Amelia," said Sheridan, when she had a little recovered from the shock she had received from the contents of the letter. "It is quite clear now to me, that you think more of this soldier than you would before admit."

"I am affected at such a communication from him," she replied. "What can it all mean?"

"I think I have a key to the mystery, and I may take it upon myself to say that you need be under no sort of apprehension whatever, on his account."

"Indeed."

"Yes, indeed. The fact is, I have, I am afraid, been the cause of this trouble that the young soldier is in, but the only reparation I can make him, is to get him out of it as quickly as I can, and that I will do, you may depend, so think no more of it, and I beg you will not put me to the blush for myself by asking any further particulars."

"Well, I will say no more about it, but rest with confidence upon your promise to see that he is saved from the fate he speaks of, which, to my mind, certainly presents itself in a dreadful shape. Mr. —a—a—a—"

"Tattam, miss," said the drummer. "Tattam is my name."

"Then, Mr. Tattam, will you go back at once to your comrade, and tell him that he need have no fear?"

"I will, miss—I will. Lord bless me, I don't think I shall ever get the better of the crush I had when that gentleman was thrown into bed on top of me, miss, and what's the oddest thing about it, is that it has made me so horribly thirsty that I do believe I could drink almost any-thing that could be offered to me."

There was no such thing as mistaking this appeal, and Amelia gave orders that he should have whatever he liked at the bar, for she was now the mistress of the place, and looked upon as such; since her aunt had fled, and her uncle was so evidently incapable of taking any part in the management of the tavern.

"Tattam," whispered Sheridan to the drummer, before he left the house, "what has Atter-bury done?"

"Don't know, sir, but he's to get three hundred lashes this morning."

"This morning?"

"Yes, sir, at twelve o'clock, unless somebody can do something for the poor fellow with his colonel. It's a sad thing, sir; for a better tempered fellow never breathed than he is; and I'm sure and certain, sir, and he'd blow his brains out with his own musket rather than he would submit to such a punishment."

"Very well. You may depend that somebody will do something for him, and that soon too; so go and tell him to keep up his spirits, and not on any account to think of anything rash."

"I will, sir. Right about, face, and I'm off. Good morning to you, sir; and I will say this much, that the brandy-and-water at this tavern is the real thing. A-hem! Capital!"

"Very well. On some other occasion you shall taste it again. Good morning to you now."

The drummer took his departure, and Sheridan, after advising Amelia to keep her uncle quiet, and to say nothing to any strangers about what had happened, left the tavern himself, and as he did so he said—

"The first thing I have to do is to rescue my friend, Atterbury, from the awkward scrape I have got him into by causing him to meet Brummel in the park. There has been some under-hand dealing in the business, I am quite certain, or else the message of the prince ought to have settled it."

Perhaps if any one had wished particularly to find where the prince was sleeping on that night, there were very few people in London who could have given the requisite information, but among that few was Sheridan.

He knew where, at all events, out of two or three places, to find him; and although it was an hour in the morning at which master George would have as little thought of rising as he would of trying to earn his living, yet his old crony under the circumstances did not scruple to disturb him.

As good luck would have it, he found him at the house of a Mr. Denny, in Old Palace Yard, where he used not unfrequently to sleep, and where there was always a bed at his disposal, and to which house he had the means of letting himself in at any hour.

It struck five as Sheridan rung a peal at the bell of the mansion.

He was answered by a half-asleep servant, who had risen to light the fire, and in answer to the question, if Mr. Brown (which was the name the prince went by to the domestics) was sleeping there, he got an answer in the affirmative, and being well known, he was at once per-mitted to go up stairs.

It was a large, old-fashioned, rambling house, and the two rooms—dressing and bed rooms—that were always ready for Mr. Brown, were upon the first floor, and very handsomely got up in the way of furniture and general fittings.

The door of the dressing room, which came first to hand, was not fast, and Sheridan at once entered it, and making his way into the inner apartment, drew aside the heavy curtains from the window, with a rattle of all its brass rings, that awakened the sleeper, who called out hastily—

"What's that? who's that?"

"Who else," said Sheridan, "but some enemy to kings, who has come with hostile intent to a paragraph in the 'Times' newspaper that will convulse Europe."

"The devil!—what?—what!—oh, confound you; why it's you, Sherry! Why what in the name of all that's wonderful has brought you here at such a time,—why what's the time?"

"The witching hour of five."

"Five? What five in the morning?"

"Exactly; but you have seen five in the morning before now."

"Yes, but I have not got out of my bed to do so."

"Nor need you do so now, for I have only come to you to ask you to write a note, which I know you will do, as it is for an act of kindness and justice that you are asked to do it. You, will no doubt, recollect that you sent a message by one Captain Strangeways to the colonel of one of the regiments of the Guards, to look over a little *fracas* that had taken place in the park between a young soldier and Brummel ?"

"Ah, to be sure—a capital joke."

"Well, it has turned out no such jest to the poor fellow, for it has been tortured into a military offence, and he is this morning to receive three hundred lashes."

"What, notwithstanding my message? Surely such a small favour might have been awarded to me."

"Don't be too hasty in taking that view of the question George. Your message must have settled the affair, had it been delivered; but I think there has been some juggling in the matter. I happen to know that the young soldier caned Brummel, and so do you likewise, and happen to know that this Captain Strangeways, who was attempted, if you recollect, to be pushed among us one morning, is not the most unscrupulous fellow in the world—in fact, he is a Scotch adventurer, and——"

"Oh, I'll get up directly—confound them all!"

"Nay, there is no occasion; Colonel Curry is a gentleman; give me a note to him, and I will go myself to the barracks and ascertain all about it."

"Very well. But if I find that Brummel has been at any underhand work in this affair, I am done with him from this day forth. I cannot and will not bear it."

Writing materials were in the room, and the following note, (still in preservation) was written to Colonel Curry of the regiment of the foot Guards to which Atterbury belonged :—

"The Prince of Wales's compliments to Colonel Curry, and would beg the favour of his looking over any fault of Thomas Atterbury, for which he is incurring military punishment, as he, the P. of Wales, takes upon himself the whole blame of the transaction, it having originated in a jest."

"George," said Sheridan, when this little note was folded up and sealed, "George, when your follies, your extravagances, your luxuries, and your magnificence are all forgotten, some little things, such as this that you have done, will live in the wreck of memory, and preserve you to a noble futurity of popularity."

"Oh, oh—very well. Now be off, and when we meet to-day, you can tell me all about it, you know. Good night—I mean good morning. Be off with you."

"I have the honour to bid you good morning, and it is an honour on such an occasion as this."

Sheridan lost no time, but at once proceeded to the barracks in the park, where he knew the regiment of Tom Atterbury was stationed; and upon arriving at the gate, he was, of course, stopped by the sentinel, who, however, allowed him to pass to the guard-house, upon his saying that he came to visit the colonel.

When there, he was obliged to give his card, and he wrote underneath his name the words—

"On urgent business."

This card was taken to the colonel, who was by no means a drawing-room soldier; but was rising, although it was not above half-past six; and he sent back his compliments to say that he would be happy to see Mr. Sheridan in his rooms at once.

The colonel occupied a handsome suite of four rooms in the barracks, and when Sheridan entered, he found him ready to receive him, while a substantial breakfast was being laid in the adjoining room.

"Pray, sir, be seated," said the colonel. "This is an unexpected honour."

"You are very kind, colonel," said Sheridan, and the spirit of fun got at the moment the better of any other feeling, as he added, "the fact is, I have come to breakfast with you."

"I am delighted to hear it, sir. Robert—Robert!"

"Yes, sir," said a soldier in undress, making his appearance.

"Robert, see what can be done in the shape of a good breakfast this morning; I have a distinguished guest; and tell your wife to go to my lady's room and say that the great, the learned and the witty Mr. Sheridan breakfasts with us, and beg her to lose no time about her toilette."

Sheridan laughed as he said—

"Colonel, you think now I have come here to perpetrate some practical joke, and you are paying me off in my own coin as we go on."

"By no means, sir—by no means. I never had a practical joke played off against me in my life. I consider, from your position, Mr. Sheridan, you may call upon any gentleman, and say—'Sir, if it be agreeable to you I have come to take breakfast with you;' and as for fancying for one moment that anything was meant beyond that, I consider that, by so doing, I should be insulting you and lowering myself."

Sheridan laughed again.   It was as clear to him as anything could possibly be, that the colonel fancied some practical joke was in progress, and that he had made up his mind it should not come off at his expense, be it of what character it might.   This was not exactly the state of things which Sheridan wished to produce, so he determined upon bringing the affair to a different complexion.

CHAPTER XXV.

CAPTAIN STRANGEWAYS FINDS HOW DIFFICULT IT IS TO RUN WITH THE HARE, AND HOLD WITH THE HOUNDS.

" Sir," said Sheridan, rising, " I have come here on too serious a business to be trifled with any longer.   Indeed, I ought not to have trifled with it at all."

The colonel bowed, as much as to say, " Certainly not."

" May I ask you a question, colonel ?"

" Of course; as many as you like."   And then he added, with a smile, " The answer, you know, is quite another affair."

" Oh, but you will answer this.   Did you receive a message from the Prince of Wales, through Captain Strangeways, to the effect that he, the prince, wished you would oblige him by looking over a little matter that had occurred in your regiment, in which a young man named Atterbury was concerned ?"

" Certainly not.   Captain Strangeways brought such a message from Mr. Brummel; and however magnanimous I might think that gentleman, I could not accede to the request."

" Mr. Brummel !"

" Yes, Mr. Brummel, who was assaulted.   But Captain Strangeways added that the assault was so unprovoked an one, that he had great difficulty in getting Mr. Brummel to say so much; and, in fact, led me to believe that he had extorted as much from him."

" And so you were not induced to pardon the man ?   Was it a military crime ?"

" Yes, and expressly provided for.   Any soldier committing an offence within a certain circuit round his barracks, is guilty of a military crime by so doing, as well as a civil one if it be one which the civil laws take cognizance of."

" Well, colonel, I was present when the prince sent by Captain Strangeways his compliments to you, and a request that you would not do anything in Atterbury's case."

" Indeed !   I had no such message.   Robert, Robert !"

" Yes, sir."

" Just go to Captain Strangeways' room, give him my compliments, and ask him to come to me directly, if convenient."

The soldier went on his errand, and while he was gone, some observations were made by Sheridan of a casual nature, for he did not wish to prejudice the case of Captain Strangeways, who was thus, no doubt, so very unexpectedly summoned upon his defence.

" Eh, what," said the captain, who was dressing, to the colonel's servant.   " The colonel wants me ?"

" Yes, sir, a gentleman has called upon the colonel, and he wishes to see you."

" Give my compliments, and say I will be with him directly.   Ah," said Strangeways to himself, when he was alone, " I guess what it is, my friend Brummel has been as good as his word, and has got me some promotion, which has been reported to the colonel.   I am, at all events, I should think, put upon the staff of the Commander-in-Chief, till a regiment turns up for me."

With such satisfactory feelings he completed his toilette, and hastened to the colonel's quarter, assuming such a smirking air of self-confidence and congratulation as was quite delightful to look upon.

" Good morning, colonel ; you did me the honour to send for me."

" Oh, no honour, Captain Strangeways, no honour—allow me to introduce you to Mr. Sheridan."

" Oh, I think I have before had the pleasure."

" Certainly not," said Sheridan, " I was never introduced to you yet, sir.   I certainly saw you at Mr. Brummel's one morning at breakfast."

" Yes—oh, yes, certainly; how is Mr. Brummel ?"

" I don't know."

"Captain Strangeways," said the colonel, " the Prince of Wales complains——"

"The—the—who ?"

"The Prince of Wales complains that he sent me a message by you, which you did not deliver. Now, you must be aware that the prince is a colonel in the army, and so your neglecting his orders is a military offence."

"Why, I—I really don't recollect that I—I—what about?"

"Sir," said Sheridan, " I was present when the prince sent a message, of a plain and simple understandable natur, to Colonel Curry by you, and I must say that I am quite amazed to find that it has not been delivered."

"I—I thought it was Mr. Brummel, who sent his compliments to—to look over Atterbury's affair."

"But that, captain, may not be the subject of the prince's complaint at all," said Colonel Curry, looking full in the face of the discomfited captain, who saw too late how he had in his hurry to make an endeavour to exculpate himself, only floundered so much deeper into the mire.

He was silent.

"Captain Strangeways," said the colonel, " Robert will show you out of my apartments, and if you can conveniently change out of my regiment into some other, I shall be much obliged."

"A man may forget a message," said the captain.

"But not falsify it, sir," said Sheridan.

"You shall answer for that word," said Strangeways.

"Willingly—but at present I have other business on hand—Colonel Curry, I have the honour of handing you a note from the prince, and bidding you good morning, with many apologies for having intruded upon you in the way I did."

"Apologies! Sir, I will not take one now; indeed, I feel that I am offended—deeply offended."

"Oh, indeed!—an offence," said Strangeways, pricking up his ears.

"Yes, you invited yourself to breakfast, Mr. Sheridan, and then talk of going away without partaking of it ; and if that is not an offence, I don't know what is."

"Then I will stay."

"Well, gentlemen," said Strangeways, " this seems to have been all a mistake, and we may as well forget it. I will write a note of apology to his royal highness."

"Robert."

"Yes, Colonel."

"Go to the captain of the guard, and say that Thomas Atterbury is to return to duty forthwith. Step this way, Mr. Sheridan ; I dare say the breakfast is laid by this time, and my wife is waiting for us to officiate. This way, if you please, Mr. Sheridan."

They both walked into the adjoining room; and as the colonel was last, he just turned round in time to shut the door bang in Captain Strangeway's face, who otherwise, with all the perseverance of a Scotchman, who has an object dear to his interest at stake, would regularly have pushed himself in, despite the repulses he had already met with, and which ought to have been quite sufficient to assure him that his company was anything but wanted at the colonel's breakfast table.

To his great surprise and immense gratification, Tom Atterbury was informed that he was free, and to go on duty again as if nothing had happened.

"But how has it come about ?" he said.

"I don't know," replied Robert; " all I am aware of is, that a gentleman has brought a letter from the Prince of Wales."

"The deuce he did.—Oh, Amelia—Amelia !"

"Oh, who ?"

"Nothing—nothing. If any of you will shoot me through the head, I shall take it as a most especial favour. I can guess how I am protected. Oh, Amelia—Amelia, how could you have interest in such a quarter. Wretched, wretched man that I am, will nobody shoot me?"

The comrades of Atterbury could not make out what it was that ailed him, for they considered that he was a wonderfully lucky fellow to escape the punishment which they had all thought he was as certain to receive as that the sun would rise, on the day that had been set apart for its infliction. But since the supposed assignation of Amelia in the park with Beau Brummel, poor Atterbury was in a state of mind to believe almost anything to the prejudice of her whom he loved.

The breakfast at the colonel's quarters passed off as pleasantly as any breakfast possibly could. The colonel's lady was a lady, and as Sheridan could, when he chose, be a perfect gentleman, he did so choose upon this occasion, and quite enchanted his entertainers with the versatility of his genius.

He told them some anecdotes most inimitably; and, indeed, two hours passed away before they thought one quarter of the time had been swallowed up in the past, and then it was only the drum beating for morning parade, that awoke the colonel to the necessity of getting ready for his official duties.

Sheridan rose instantly.

"Well, sir," said the colonel, "I shall always look back with pleasure to this morning, and I only hope that you will not wait until you have another letter to deliver, before you come again."

"I shall be most happy," said the colonel's lady, "to make breakfast for Mr. Sheridan, whenever he may honour me by coming to partake of it."

"I don't know that I dare come again."

"Not dare! Why not, Mr. Sheridan?"

"Madam, there are some books that I have read once—some pictures and some natural scenery that I have seen once—some strains of music that I have heard once—and they have left so complete a charm on my memory, such a beautiful spell over their recollections, that I find it one of my greatest pleasures to know I have such idols, and that I may approach them when I please, but abstain from doing so."

"Never mind that," said the colonel, "you must come; mind, we shall expect you within a week at the outside. Do you think I ought to write to the prince?"

"Oh no, I will tell him all about it. There is no occasion to write at all. Madam, good morning. I am going now from a shrine out again into the world, that will contrast strangely with the last two hours, but not more changed shall I be than it is. I have a terrible facility of mental adaptation to circumstances, and when you see some one shake his head gravely over some escapade of Sheridan's, do not believe that it is Sheridan the man, who has so committed himself, but Sheridan the mimic, who saw somebody else being a little vicious, and carried out his unfortunate propensity by imitating so very bad an example. Madam, once more adieu."

CHAPTER XXVI.

A DARK MEETING.

WHEN Lord Marchmont got to his hotel after the little incident at the lawyer's chambers, at Gray's Inn, he felt all those uncomfortable sensations which are likely to come over a man when he has done some act which the apparently urgent necessity to do, does not at all rob of its disagreeables.

He flung himself upon a couch, and gave such a groan, that his valet was really alarmed, and would certainly have at once sent for a physician, but for his master's point blank "No," when such a course was proposed to him.

"Ruined, ruined," moaned Lord Marchmont. "Undone quite."

"May I be permitted," said the valet, who, knowing his master's difficulties, and having been very faithful to him, now and then indulged in the liberty of asking a question, and giving his opinion, "may I be permitted to hope, my lord, that nothing fresh of a disagreeable nature has occurred."

"Uncommonly fresh," said Marchmont.

"Ahem! May I inquire—what——"

"Oh, yes. I am going to marry."

"Marry! marry! Who?"

"The devil, for all I know, my good fellow. It's of no use to stare in that way, and look so panic-struck, it is as good as done. I am going to be married, and there's an end of it."

"Your lordship is much mistaken in thinking that there's an end of it. I was married once, and I rather think, my lord, I ought to know pretty well."

"It's of no use arguing the matter, it's done."

"No, my lord; a man cannot be said to be thoroughly done till he is married, you know, and I take upon myself, of course, to say that such is not your lordship's case. Affairs sometimes look much more desperate than they really are. Come, cheer up, my lord, we have together weathered many a gale of evil fortune, and I don't see why we should give in to this one, whatever it may chance to be all about. Cheer up, my lord, cheer up."

"I cannot. Hark, what's that?"

"The waiter with a letter for your lordship. That will do, William, I'll hand it to his lordship. Shall I read it to you, my lord?—you have had that confidence in me."

"Ah, do—do."

The valet opened the letter, and with a preparatory hem! read as follows:—

"GRAY'S INN.

"MY LORD,—I have the honour of writing to your lordship to say that *the* lady hearing from me that your lordship was anxious for an interview, will grant one upon certain conditions.—Firstly, that the interview should take place in a darkened room; and secondly, that you will give your word of honour as a gentleman to make no attempt to see or detain the lady, who is

willing that you should come to some judgment concerning her by conversation, but nothing more.

"Should such a proceeding be agreeable to your lordship, and you will oblige by sending a not signifying so much, and then call at the chambers as above at eight o'clock this evening, tho arrangement can and will, anything hereinbefore contained to the contrary in anywise notwithstandin., be carried out. "I have the honour to be, my lord,

"Your lordship's most obedient servant,

"JOHN BOYNE."

"To LORD MARCHMONT.'

No. 10.

There was a death-like silence of some three or four minutes' duration in the room, after the valet had read this rather extraordinary epistle, for he could make nothing of it, and it was both annoying and perplexing to Lord Marchmont.

"Confound the fellow, and all lawyers with him," said Marchmont, at length.

"Amen!" said the valet. "Can your lordship throw any light on this extraordinary epistle?"

"Oh, it's about my wife that is to be—that's all."

"Then—then, my lord, you have not even seen her, and if I may make such a bull, the first interview is to be in the dark, where you can get no view at all. Is that it, my lord, really?"

"That's about it, Stevens."

"I'm all amazement. Why, my lord, she may have two wooden legs—false teeth—glass eyes, and a cork——"

"Peace—peace—she may have what she likes, and be what she likes—I am to marry her. It comes to that, and be hanged to her, you, and all the world beside. I am a desperate man."

"So I should say, my lord."

"Hark you! go to the chambers of that lawyer, and say I shall be there at eight o'clock, and—do you hear me, Stevens?"

"Yes, my lord, as well as a man can be supposed to hear whose ears have been so blasted by such a piece of information as I have had just now from your lordship."

"Well, well, no more of that. But you used to be a skilful hand at finding out any secret. You soon found out all mine."

"Your lordship does me too much honour."

"So you will find a boy at that lawyer's chambers whom they name Peter. See if you cannot pump something out of him. I should think that by dint of prying and listening, he surely must know more of this affair than I do. Try your luck, Stevens, and let me find you the clever fellow I always thought you."

"Will your lordship favour me with all the particulars?"

"Oh, yes, yes."

Lord Marchmont then told his valet all that the reader is already aware of, concerning the extraordinary projected marriage, and in the course of half an hour Mr. Stevens was en route to Gray's-inn on his pumping expedition to the immaculate Peter.

Stevens fully merited every possible encomium that his master could give to him, for his great judgment, and particularly his most admirable tact in finding out other people's affairs, at which, perhaps, like a number of other very clever people, he laboured far more assiduously than at his own.

When he reached Gray's-inn, he assumed a careless nonchalant air, as if nothing of any importance engaged him, and he ascended the dull, dirty stairs, leading to the chambers of Mr. Boyne, slowly, so that he should not lack breath at all when he reached the top. A slight tap brought Peter to the door at once.

"Is Mr. Boyne at home?" was the first question propounded.

"No," said Peter, "and won't be for some time."

"Oh, ah. Well, you have so much the appearance of a gentleman—a lad of parts and wit, that I am sure I may quite safely say to you what I have to say."

"Oh, yes—you may say anything to me—what is it?"

"Lord Marchmont, then, will be here at eight."

"Really."

"You don't seem at all to care about it, I should say—didn't you know he was expected at that hour?"

"Not I, and I don't see that it matters much to me, one way or the other, it's much the same whether he comes or not—is that all you have got to say, old fellow? if it is, I'll shut the door again."

"Well, it is not quite all, in a manner of speaking, I may remark. First and foremost, I may as well say that I am rather thirsty or so."

"Thirsty, I'm always thirsty, and the great bore is, that I can never get anybody to treat me to anything."

"That don't apply in the present instance, then, for I'll treat you, so come on—I suppose you know where a drop of something is to be got decent about here?"

"Rather."

Peter in a minute put a little ticket on the door, which announced that he would return instantly, and then shutting up the chambers, he accompanied Mr. Stevens to a choice tap in the neighbourhood, where they imbibed, at the expense of Stevens, divers fluids of an exciting character, before the valet thought it was prudent to propound any of the questions he was charged with to Peter, from whom he certainly hoped to obtain some substantial and accurate information to his master.

"Ah—Peter, I think your name is," he said.

"Yes, that's about it, Peter Marrow is my name."

"What an odd name, Marrow; well, Peter Marrow—take another drop—oh, don't spare it, and, Peter Marrow, as I was saying, this is rather an odd affair—this marriage between the Lord Marchmont and a lady of whom he really knows nothing at all—don't spare the glass, Peter, I'm forced to be abstemious, but don't you spare it on any account."

"Thank you, thank you, I won't; and, as you say, this marriage affair is very curious—perhaps you can give me some information about it."

"What! I—I thought, of course, that you knew all about it, living with Mr. Boyne; I, of course, thought that you were the very man to know all the particulars. Take another glass."

"No objection to another glass, Mr. What's-your-name, but if I know anything about the affair, may I be hanged."

"Then you are a fool. Good day—you are an ass!"

CHAPTER XXVII.

A MYSTERIOUS VISITOR AT THE WHEATSHEAF.

LET us have a peep at Mr. Booker.

Alas, poor Booker! he must have loved the Widow Mortimer, or a knowledge of who and what she was could never have affected him to the extent it did. She was a fine woman, certainly, and with the one little exception of trying to hurry him out of this world a little sooner than he felt inclined to go, or that in the ordinary course of events he would have gone, her conduct to him, Mr. Booker, had been exemplary—yes, quite exemplary.

What a pity such a woman should give her mind to poisoning by wholesale. What a pity that there should be little green bottles, with insinuating liquids in them.

But to return to Mr. Booker, whom we certainly left in anything but a satisfactory state for any gentleman to be in, who is so much entitled to our regard as he is. He slept for a considerable time, and then, when he awoke, Amelia sat down by his bedside and bespoke his serious attentions to what she had to say.

This he promised to do, but she only just stopped him in time as he was about to say something about being better after his brandy-and-water.

"Uncle," said she, "something very serious has occurred; Mrs. Booker overheard Mr. Sheridan telling you about her conduct, and as a consequence, she escaped at once; I am not exactly prepared to say that I am sorry it is so. Perhaps all is for the best, uncle, but what I wish you now to do is, to make up your mind what you mean to do for the future."

"My mind!" said poor Booker, and he said the words in such a helpless way that they conveyed most painfully to Amelia how much that mind was shattered by what had taken place.

"Yes, uncle, have you any plans?"

"Oh dear no, child, I have no plans! Perhaps I shall be better after my brandy-and-water."

"Uncle, uncle, do not repeat that phrase; whenever you do, it will, you may depend, have a tendency to bring your thoughts back to the most unpleasant circumstances which have recently occurred!"

"Well, I won't."

"Then, uncle, will you make up your mind to go to the country, and be quiet and happy?"

"Yes, oh dear, yes. Anything for quietness and brandy-and-water."

"Get up, then, uncle, and come down to the bar-room as soon as you can, for I am going out a short distance, and it is requisite that in the house there should be some person of authority."

He looked at her for a moment with a puzzled air, and then he said—

"My dear, excuse me, I thought you were something of a—a—fool. But now you really seem to be quite the reverse of that. How is that, Amelia?"

"This is one of the mysteries of those affairs, uncle, that I will explain to you by-and-by; promise me that you will be down stairs shortly, if you can."

"Oh, yes; reach me my—my——"

"You can help yourself, I dare say, uncle," said Amelia with a laugh, as she tripped out of the room, "without my assistance, and mind, I am waiting for you."

"Yes, my dear, yes. I'll recollect that, I will come directly. Perhaps I shall be better after my brandy-and-water."

Mr. Booker was as good as his word, for in about twenty minutes he came down to the bar-parlour, and although he looked a little confused, like a man who has had ugly dreams, he certainly was very much recovered in comparison to what he had been when he was first taken to bed by Mr. Sheridan and Tom the pot-boy.

A very short time now saw Mr. Booker in the bar-parlour, and sitting in the identical seat from whence, but a short time before, the Widow Mortimer was wont to issue her mandates to the household.

Amelia thought that perhaps a little of the brandy-and-water business would not be altogether amiss in effecting the complete restoration of her uncle, so she had a glass mixed for him, and, placing it at his elbow, she said—

"Now, uncle, I shall not be long, and you had better throw aside sorrow, and make yourself as comfortable as you can."

"I will, my dear."

"That's right, and who knows but what all that has happened may, after all, be for the best."

"Ah," said Mr. Booker, "who knows?" and then, in a sort of abstracted manner, he added, "perhaps he will be better after his brandy-and-water."

Amelia did not hear the latter part of the remark of her uncle, or she might have suspected he was not so much recovered as she had thought and hoped, and she would probably have placed him much closer under the surveillance of Maria than she did, for she merely told her to attend to Mr. Booker if he wanted anything.

There sat the disconsolate seventh husband, then, of the Widow Mortimer, slowly sipping the brandy-and-water, and in about as complete a state of mental confusion as any gentleman could expect to be in, let what would happen.

"It's horrid," he muttered to himself, "but I always knew from the first moment that I heard of the other six fellows, that something dreadful would be the end of it. Heigho! I have all their names down in my pocket-book."

As he spoke, he produced a small pocket-book, and, opening it at a leaf which, from its soiled aspect, would appear to have been often consulted, he continued—

"Ah, here they all are: I put them down while the names were quite fresh in my memory. What a dreadful list for a husband to read—Mortimer, Lee, Luton, Fiddler, Brown, and Green. I wonder what sort of a man Fiddler was?"

Just as Mr. Booker had finished this catalogue of the Widow Mortimer's husbands, and was looking up to the ceiling in a contemplative way, wondering what sort of a man the deceased Mr. Fiddler was, he was startled by hearing some one pronounce his name.

"Mr. Booker."

"Yes—yes! what! who is it? Perhaps he will be better after his brandy-and-water," exclaimed Mr. Booker, partially relapsing from a sort of conviction that something else was about to happen of an alarming and exciting character.

"Mr. Booker," said the voice again, and then Booker, as he looked in the direction from whence the sound came, saw a rather gentlemanly looking personage leaning over the little hatch of the bar.

"Mr. Booker," again said the voice, "I have something to say to you."

"Well," said Booker, with unwonted mental power, "why don't you say it?—I was wondering what sort of man Mr. Fiddler was."

"Indeed," said the stranger, as he reached his hand over the half-door, and in a manner that showed he must have been well accustomed to the lock inside it.

"Yes—yes—yes—who are you?"

"That I will soon let you know. I hope you are in tolerable good health, Mr. Booker."

There was a something now and then only about the tones of the stranger, which made Booker think he must have heard the voice somewhere before; but it was only occasionally that such a reminiscence came across him, and he could not for the life of him think where he had heard those tones.

"Yes," he said, "I am pretty well," and then again he added, "who are you?"

"Why, to tell the truth," said the stranger, "my name is not often pronounced; it's rather a secret."

"Is it really?"

"Yes. But you pronounced it; and that was what gave me power, as I was hovering about the spot, to show myself to you, as I have now done."

"Power—hovering—what—what do you mean?"

"Incline your ear, Mr. Booker, and don't let it go any further. But I am what was—Fiddler."

"The devil!"

"Oh, no—no. There you do me an injustice; I am the apparition of Fiddler; but you see there is nothing repulsive in my appearance; nothing that you need at all avoid, Mr. Booker. I have come, not to alarm you, but to ask you, as you are the last husband of widow Mortimer, to do me a favour, which you can do very easily in this house."

The hair almost stood on end on poor Booker's head as these words were said to him; and it was some moments before he could gasp out—

"What! what is it you wish me to do, Mr. Fiddler—what, oh, what is it?"

"You will oblige me by going up to your bed-room, and opening a cupboard, which is in a corner by the right hand side of the bed's head, and bringing to me a small mahogany box, which is upon the top shelf."

"You—you seem to know the place well."

"Of course I do know it as well as you do, or as Green, or Brown, or Lee, or Mortimer, or Luton knew it. Go and do as I ask of you, and you will be entitled to my gratitude instead of—but no matter; I know you will oblige me"

"Yes—yes. It's a small matter, Mr.—a—a—Fiddler."

"Then go at once."

Poor Booker, now more thoroughly bewildered than ever, rose and trotted from the bar-parlour more like a man walking in his sleep than anything else. He slowly ascended the stairs till he reached the bed-room; and then opening the cupboard which had been mentioned, he sure enough found upon the top shelf of it, just such a box as the representative of the deceased Mr. Fiddler had mentioned to him, and desired to be possessed of.

It was an ordinary enough looking box, and by the slight shake which Mr. Booker gave to it, seemed to him to contain papers and nothing else. Clutching it firmly in his hands, he slowly and tremblingly descended the stairs with it.

There, seated still in the bar-parlour, was the apparition—it could not be a dream. The whole affair was too clear and consistent for that. No, he thought to himself, it is a dreadful reality. One of the frightful circumstances attendant upon the whole affair of his marriage with the widow Mortimer. And yet how very terrific it was to think of, that he should be carrying a box to the ghost of Mr. Fiddler, the Fiddler who had been poisoned.

"Is—is that it?" gasped Booker.

"It is," said the apparition. "It is it. Give it to me, Mr. Booker. Thank you: and now, farewell, probably for ever."

He took the little mahogany box from the unresisting hands of Mr. Booker, and in another moment left him alone in the bar, although whether the ghost walked out, glided out, or disappeared up through the ceiling, or down through the floor, poor Booker was in by far too great mental confusion to be at all able to say.

He shot off his chair, and rolling down upon the floor, as he was accustomed to do when in circumstances of great perplexity, muttered—

"He'll be bettter after his brandy-and-water."

CHAPTER XXVIII.

THE MEETING IN THE DARK CHAMBERS BETWEEN THE HAPPY PAIR.

WE very much, of course, regret the direful necessity of leaving poor Booker in so desperate a state of mind and body as he is in now, but other interests compel us to do so.

We feel that we are bound forthwith to acquaint our readers with how Lord Marchmont got through his singular interview with his intended wife, in the dark.

In Turkey a happy bridegroom, except by chance of some monstrous infringement of custom, sees nothing of his bride until he lifts the veil from before her features, when she has become his property, and it would seem that this custom had charms for the daughter of the Mr. Smith, since she did not feel disposed to admit his lordship to see her until after the ceremony.

Probably, however, she possessed some extraordinary and fascinating powers of mind, which induced her to think that she could, by a little conversation induce a strong feeling in her favour.

But be Miss Smith's feelings what they might in the business, one thing was perfectly clear, and that was, that the Lord Marchmont's were anything but of a pleasant character.

He felt himself, as indeed he was, a man who had got into the inextricable toils of a set of circumstances, from which there was no escape. He was in debt!

Yes, in debt, and that one word is quite sufficient, in a mammon-loving community like this, to comprise every evil under the sun.

There was he, Lord Marchmont, a nobleman, the intimate of a prince—a man, too, of considerable expectations, actually forced into a match with one whom he had never seen. Oh, omnipotent power of creditors over debtors.

As eight o'clock approached, the hour at which, it will be recollected, he was to be introduced to the lady, his uneasiness became very great.

Then again, the ill-success of his valet in getting any information had tended to annoy him, although that individual had not told exactly how he had been foiled by Peter, whom he suspected very much of having a laugh at his expense.

"You could get nothing out of him, Stevens?" said Lord Marchmont.

"Nothing, my lord. The fool knows nothing."

"I thought differently from that."

"Oh, dear no, my lord. He knows nothing at all. If he had known anything at all, your lordship doesn't suppose that I should have been long in finding it out?"

"I know your abilities, Stevens, and I can easily enough suppose that, on such an occasion as this, you would see the propriety of exerting them."

"Certainly, my lord; I got the fellow into such a line, that if he had committed a murder I, am quite sure that I should have come away as a depository of the secret of where the dead body of his victim was hidden. But he knows nothing."

"And consequently could tell nothing."

"Exactly, my lord."

"Well, Stevens, there was a sort of negative merit in that, you know; for I have always found, that when you know nothing, you take good care to invent something, rather than your abilities should be called in question."

"Oh, your lordship is by far too complimentary."

Lord Marchmont could not laugh at anything. His mind was by far too full of his own affairs, and although the prospect they embraced was one which abstractedly he would have hailed with delight—namely, the freedom from debt and pecuniary liability, yet was that piece of happiness associated with so terrific an evil, in the shape of his marriage with the usurer's daughter, Miss Smith, that he actually trembled when he thought of it.

Perhaps, even then he would have done anything and dared anything to escape from the affair, out that whenever he began to think of such a course, there came across his mind the horrible recollection of the abominable written promise of marriage that he had signed."

"Oh!" he would groan, "if it were not for that, I could perhaps defy them yet."

"What, my lord?" said Stevens, after overhearing this remark at least a dozen times.

"Nothing—nothing. There, go and get me a coach, I must go out to keep this accursed appointment at Gray's Inn. I wish Gray's Inn, and all the lawyers in it, were smothered.

"Amen! my lord. I wish so, likewise, most devoutly. I too, my lord, have had my wrongs, and some other day, when your lordship's mind is quite easy, and you have nothing to think of, and nothing to vex you, I will tell you."

"When such a state of things as that occurs, Stevens, you may tell me just what you like, but if you wait till then, I am pretty confident that not in this world will you be ever doomed to make to me such a confession."

"Oh, don't despair, my lord."

"There, there, go and get me a coach at once, I want none of your mock condolence. I am, as it were, at war with fortune; and the jade is evidently determined to make me feel that she can get the better of me in the conflict."

A coach was duly procured, into which his lordship stepped with a heavy heart, and was soon driven to Gray's Inn, to keep his appointment with his unknown bride, that was to be.

If ever a man had an uncomfortable drive of about half an hour in an old ricketty, wheezy dirty looking coach, that man was Lord Marchmont. Yes, actually a lord; one of those favoured mortals, pointed out by fortune to have a handle to his name, who should excite the envy and admiration of the profane multitude.

Truly all is not gold that glitters.

When he arrived at the chambers of the attorney, he was received by Peter with that kind of look which seemed to say—you are expected, and we are all ready for you. He was at once ushered into the private room of Mr. Boyne, in which a couple of tall candles were burning upon the table, and shedding a very tolerable light upon all subjects within the apartment.

There was an odious kind of leer upon the lawyer's face.

"Well, sir," said Lord Marchmont, "you see I am here to my appointment."

"You are, my lord, and to your time likewise," was the reply. "Believe me, my lord, this condescension on the part of your lordship is duly appreciated both by myself and by the lady."

"Is she here?"

"She will be here," replied the attorney, somewhat evasively. "She will be here, my lord,

Allow me to say that, with the most implicit reliance upon your lordship's word of honour, you will make no attempt whatever to disturb the incognito of the lady; I will now leave you to enjoy your interview at your leisure."

"Enjoy!" muttered Lord Marchmont; but the lawyer thought that he spoke interrogatively, and hastened at the moment to reply, with something of a sneer in his tone—

"Surely, my lord, it must be a great and a genuine enjoyment to have an opportunity of uninterrupted converse with her ladyship that is to be. I should fancy it really the very highest of all pleasures."

"I did not ask for your opinion."

"Good, my lord, I will no longer detain you."

He rose as he spoke, and with all the deliberation in the world, snuffed out one of the lights.

"Why, what are you about now?"

"I am quite surprised, my lord, at your asking such a question. I am, of course, preparing for your meeting the lady; and as that meeting is to be in the dark, it seems to me but a necessary preliminary to it, that the light should be got rid of."

"Very well, very well," said Lord Marchmont, as he flung himself back in his seat, and made up his mind to allow Mr. Boyne to do and say just what he liked, although there was a certain air of familiar impertinence about his manner, which was by no means relished by his lordship.

Having then most carefully put out one of the lights, the attorney took the other in his hand, and moving towards the door of the room, he made a low bow, which had in it a great amount of mock reverence, and then he disappeared from before the eyes of his puzzled lordship.

There must have been some very ingenious means used for the purpose of excluding the slightest ray of light, actual or reflected, from gas light or window, from that apartment; for the darkness that Lord Marchmont found himself in was the most complete that he had ever in his life experienced.

What is called ordinarily by the name of darkness, is only obscurity, for there will come from some quarter or another a wandering ray of light, however indistinct, that will banish a portion of the blackness, although it may have no effect whatever in improving the distinctness of outlines.

But such was not the fact as concerned the darkness in which was Lord Marchmont now. It was a darkness of a most total and black terrific character—a darkness which seemed as if it could have been felt, and which left all objects in conjecture.

This state of things continued for some minutes, during which Lord Marchmont heard no sound, but the rather hurried and tumultuous beating of his own heart, for he was, despite all his exertions to the contrary, most singularly agitated at the novel circumstances in which he was placed.

As minute after minute thus passed away, his imagination began to be preternaturally active, and to play him all sorts of strange pranks. He fancied that he saw grinning faces in the air, and that huge forms, upheld by nothing, were performing horridly agile gyrations in the slack darkness that was above and around him. But still no one came, and he at last got into such a state of painful feeling, that he felt he could endure the suspense no longer.

"Speak—speak," he said, "I will remain here not another minute; if this meeting of voices is to take place at all, let it take place at once. I will endure suspense no longer."

A dismal sort of echo of his own voice was the only sound that responded to his call, and he actually trembled as he sat, partially leaning forward upon his chair, and making vain efforts to cheat himself into a belief that he heard some voice replying.

CHAPTER XXIX.

THE MEETING AND THE CHARITY BOY OF TIPPINGTON.—A VERY GREAT CHANGE INDEED.

ANOTHER five minutes, but not more than five minutes, passed away, and Lord Marchmont's patience was certainly at the lowest possible ebb—he was about to say something else, and had, in fact, actually risen from his seat for that purpose, when, amid the darkness and the stillness, there came a voice upon his ears.

The tones were quite evidently those of a person endeavouring to speak in a totally different key to what they were accustomed to, and yet there was a sweetness about them that won most irresistibly upon the ear.

"Who is here," said the voice—"who is here that wishes to speak with the unknown?"

After a moment's pause, during which Lord Marchmont was taxing his memory to find out where he had heard that voice before, and endeavouring in vain to pierce the darkness around him with his eyes, to catch a glimpse of the speaker, he replied—

"You doubtless know well enough who I am, and if you are the lady whom I came to meet, I can only offer you such compliments as a total ignorance concerning you may warrant."

"You asked for this interview," said the voice.

"Not exactly. I asked for an interview; but certainly I did not ask for an interview of so very unsatisfactory a nature as this. I merely put up with so poor a boon for want of a better."

"It is not necessary you should know more of me just at present than you do, except you achieve that knowledge by questions. You may ask me what you please, I am here to answer; but I in my turn shall ask something of you, my lord."

"Very well, madam; I dare say I shall not object to answer; and in the first instance, may I ask if you are fully aware of the conditions on which I have consented to marry?"

"I am—you are to be free from all debt from the moment that you make me your wife."

"That is it, certainly; but are you not afraid to wed a man whose affections have yet to be won by you, or who, for all you may know to the contrary, may have them already engaged?"

"No."

"Well, that is certainly a short and conclusive answer. May I then, without offence, ask if this interview in the dark is for the purpose of concealing any—any—pray excuse me, madam —any personal defect which might be revolting to my sight, and which a full knowledge of it might afterwards be as prejudicial to your happiness as to mine. Pardon me, madam, for speaking so very freely."

"Don't mention it, you have a perfect right to do so. I have no physical defects, whatever, like your lordship, my moral ones may happen to be. Are you answered?"

"I am certainly answered; but I scarcely expected such a compliment along with the answer, madam. I suppose, now I have asked all the questions I wish to ask of you, I must submit myself to answer any that you may propose?"

"I have but one."

"I am happy to hear it, madam, and I am not without a hope that the candour with which I shall reply to it may have the effect of inducing you to allow me yet, before I leave this place, to have the pleasure of seeing you as well as conversing with you."

"You may banish such an expectation, for it will not be realised."

"I regret to hear it, madam; but from the tone in which you make the remark, I can well believe that there is no hope of a contrary result."

"None whatever; and now the question I have to ask of you is one that I expect a clear and frank answer to."

"I promise such an answer."

"Is there then any just cause or impediment to prevent your contracting a marriage with me, in the shape of promise or honourable obligation to another, and have you ever played the part of the betrayer to woman's trusting affection?"

There was a death-like stillness for a moment, and when Lord Marchmont replied to this most searching question his voice was rather harsh and husky.

"Madam," he said, "I have promised to answer you candidly, and I will say, therefore, that I am no Joseph, and that I have been what is called 'a man of the world,' and I may have been engaged in gallantries."

"You have not answered me. I want to know if you ever, under the most solemn promises of faithfulness and honour, deceived the trusting heart of woman? Answer me yes or no."

"Pardon me. There are many questions which must not be answered so categorically, for if they were, they would only create a very erroneous impression; and I can only say that I have been engaged in gallantries. You as a lady, I am sure, would not wish me to descend to particulars."

"You acknowledge then, as I understand you, that you have been engaged in such a transaction. If you had not done so, I should have left you to a prison; but as you have, at least, the merit of truth, in this instance, I will condescend to save you from the results of your own extravagancies."

"Of course I am infinitely obliged," said Lord Marchmont, in a voice of sarcasm. "Is there anything else you would like to say?"

There was no answer to this; but in about half a minute he heard a door rather violently shut, and then there was to his eyes a bewildering glare of light, and the attorney stood in the room with a lighted candle in his hand.

"Where is she?" cried Marchmont, starting to his feet. "Where is she?"

"Gone, my lord, and, I should say, the coach which she has gone away in has made some progress by this time."

"Gone—gone ! The devil !"

"I hope your lordship's interview has been of a satisfactory nature."

"No, sir, it has not," said Lord Marchment ; and then, without waiting to exchange another word with the attorney, upon whose face he thought he detected a covert smile, he walked from the chambers, flung himself into the hackney coach that was in waiting for him, and directed he should be driven at once to his lodgings.

"Ha, ha !" said Mr. Boyne, when he was gone. "He don't seem to like it."

"No, that he don't," said Peter.

"How dare you make a remark, you scoundrel ! You get more and more insolent every day. I shall part with you, if you ever again dare to interpose a word. Insolence, indeed ! There are plenty of clerks, thank God, to be had for the wages I give you—seven shillings a week, as regularly as the Saturday comes round—you ungrateful rascal !—and an office fire all day in the winter to warm yourself at, too. Oh, what a world we live in !"

"So we do, Mr. Boyne."

* * * * * *

That night, at about a quarter-past ten, a hackney-coach drove up to the gate of a workhouse

No. 11.

situated about three miles to the eastward of the city, and which was called Tippington workhouse.

It was not so called on account of the place in which it was situated being named Tippington, but, when it was first projected, a wealthy parishioner had taken the whole expense upon himself, and as his name was Tippington, the workhouse was so called, in compliment to him.

It was a long, straggling, dull, unhappy-looking building, but not half so unhappy as the wretched beings who were forced to seek a permanent or temporary shelter from the storms of fate within its gloomy precincts.

The arrival of a coach, the driver of which was in handsome livery, and at the back of which was a footman redolent of gold lace, at such an hour, at the gate of Tippington workhouse, was quite an event; and the old pauper whose duty it then happened to be to play the part of gate-porter was so paralysed with astonishment, that, when the footman looked completely over his head, and asked if anybody was at home, he could not answer him.

"Come, old square toes," added the footman, "don't be staring at me, as if you never saw a gent before."

"Oh, oh," said the old man; "dear me."

"I say, is there any of the authorities here, old fellow, that a lady can speak to?"

"Please, sir, are you the Lord Mayor?"

"Why, no," said John, with a benign smile; "not exactly yet, my good man; but a lady in yon carriage has come to speak about a child that she thinks is in the workhouse."

"Oh—ah—yes, sir; I begin to understand. What—suppose, my lord, I was to wake up Mr. Ogg, the beadle?"

The footman was so well pleased to be called my lord, even by an old superannuated pauper, that he smiled twice before he could reply.

"Yes; certainly, my good man, call up Mr. Ogg. Really, the poor people here are remarkably intelligent; I may say, remarkably intelligent, considering all things—a-hem!"

Then, while the poor old pauper hobbled away to wake up the great Mr. Ogg, John went to the window of the carriage, and after touching the rim of his hat, addressed his mistress, saying—

"The beadle, ma'am, will be here directly."

"Oh! very well," said the lady; "that will do."

She was a pleasant, sweet-spoken lady, and most splendidly attired.

Now, when the poor old pauper talked of waking up Mr. Ogg, the beadle, he did not mean that that gentleman had gone to bed, but that he was in what he called his own room in the workhouse, sleeping, or rather dozing, off the effects of his evening's potations before he retired to rest, which was his habit, before eleven o'clock.

It was quite with fear and trembling that the old man entered Mr. Ogg's room, and he stood ready to make his escape as he said, in a weak, tremulous voice—

"If you please, sir, there's a lady in a carriage, as wants you."

To the old man's surprise, Mr. Ogg woke up at once, and said, in quite a gracious manner—

"All's right; she's a little after her time, that's all. Run, and say I'll be down in a minute, and go into the boy's dormitory, and bring out No. Twenty-two."

"Yes, sir—oh, yes, sir. Thank you, sir—much obliged to you, Mr. Ogg—oh, very much. What can make him be so civil, and what can he want with No. Twenty-two at this time o'night, I wonder? Ah, well, well—the longer we live, I suppose, the more we learn. Oh, dear me, my old bones ache."

The dormitory of Tippington workhouse was a huge room, in which the recipients of Tippington charity were wont to rest, upon little impracticable-looking iron bedsteads, of the most uncomfortable description, and upon which it would certainly require long practice to enable any one to catch a wink of repose.

There was a number to each of these bedsteads, so that the old pauper had no difficulty in getting hold of Twenty-two, whom he pulled out by the legs, and then told to dress himself.

Twenty-two did dress himself, and it said wonders for the kind of moral power which the authorities of Tippington workhouse had obtained over the victims submitted to their rule, that Twenty-two never asked a question as to the why or wherefore he was pulled out of bed at that time of night, and told to dress himself; but simply arrayed himself in the yellow cloth smalls, worsted stockings, shoes, and cut away coat, which was the Tippington costume, with the coolness of a Russian soldier.

Alas, poor Twenty-two, and every other numeral that had anything to do with Tippington workhouse!

In the meantime Mr. Ogg, the beadle, had found his way to the carriage-door, where he was received by the lady with a nod of recognition, by which it would appear that they were old acquaintances, and perhaps they were.

"He is here?" she said.

"Oh dear, yes, ma'am, old Anthony Pligit is a pulling him out o' bed now, ma'am. Many thanks to you, ma'am, for the bank-note as you sent."

CHAPTER XXX.

NO. TWENTY-TWO IS MADE A FINE GENTLEMAN QUITE UNEXPECTEDLY.

"Do not mention the note," said the lady; "it is of no consequence."

"Not to a lady like you, ma'am, I suppose," said Mr. Ogg, the beadle; "but to me, ma'am, as an humble beadle, it's quite another sort of thing; and I can only say as I hopes everything has been done to your satisfaction, ma'am. for these last six years."

"Quite so, if secrecy has been preserved."

"Inviolate, ma'am—inviolate."

"Then I am, of course, satisfied, for I asked no more than that, if you recollect, Mr. Ogg, and for that you have had from me——"

"Twenty pounds a year, ma'am, paid regularly—I will say that, and no mistake, ma'am, in the world, many thanks to you. But here comes Twenty-two; you will find him grown a bit, though he looks rather delicate sometimes."

The lady threw herself back in the carriage, so that her countenance was not visible, while these remarks were being made by Mr. Ogg, and in another moment the poor little charity boy was brought to the steps of the carriage.

"This is Twenty-two," said the old pauper.

"Put him into the carriage," said the lady, but they none of them saw her face then. "Put him into the carriage, John."

"Me, ma'am—me, ma'am? Me touch a charity brat? Oh dear no, ma'am. There must be some mistake."

"There will be no mistake in your leaving my service to-morrow," said the lady.

"Very good, ma'am—very good. As to leaving of your service, ma'am, that's one thing; but as to lifting charity brats into carriages, that's quite another. Lady Tumbledown will take me at once. I left my last place because I would not carry up a tray for the governess to the second floor."

No. Twenty-two, being thus discarded by John, was lifted into the carriage by Mr. Ogg, and the lady, in a clearer voice than she had hitherto spoken, said—

"Home."

The steps were condescendingly put up by John, who, when he got up behind the vehicle, told the coachman confidentially, that if he were him, he would get off the box at once, rather than suffer the indignity of driving a charity brat, and that he, John, only rode behind until they should reach a coach-stand, when he intended to avail himself of the first vehicle he could see, and so get rid of his present degrading avocation.

"Ah," said the coachman, with a sigh, "so would I, but I job the horses, you know, John, and I can't leave my cattle; you see that makes a wonderful difference to me."

"You have no soul," said John, and then he turned his back to the coachman, and held on by the straps behind the carriage, looking out for a hackney coach.

While John was thus thinking of his dignity, and the dreadful manner in which it had been wounded, No. Twenty-two was sitting in the coach, under a full impression now that he was the object of an uncommonly vivid dream. The lady was silent, so that there was nothing to disturb the idea, and when the vehicle at length stopped at a handsome house a little on the outskirts of the town, northward, Twenty-two trembled at the idea of a change coming over the spirit of his dream that might not be at all pleasant.

The door was opened by John, who had not been able to see a hackney coach, or who had thought it prudent not to hire one, and then the lady stepped out, and beckoned to No. Twenty-two to follow.

She led him across a paved hall, then up a flight of stone stairs, and so on into a room, and then into another much smaller, where there was a shaded lamp burning upon the table, and she so seated herself at the table that the light fell upon the face of No. Twenty-two, while the shadow fell upon her,

A few minutes' silence ensued, and then, as Twenty-two did not speak, she broke it by saying—

"By what name were you known at the workhouse?"

"Twenty-two."

"Nothing else than Twenty-two?—surely you were named something."

"Yes; Friday now and then, Twenty-two Friday, and sometimes a little beast."

"How old are you?"

"Don't know—don't hit me."

"Hit you! what do you mean? You are far from any ill-usage here, you may be assured of that. Do you usually get struck for nothing?"

"Oh, no; not for nothing, but for not knowing what I am asked: but may I say what I like to you, madam?"

"You may ask me what questions you like; it will be for me then to decide whether I answer them or not."

"Then I want to know if this is all a dream or not, if you please, madam; because, if it is, it will be very dreadful to awaken and find one's self in the workhouse at Tippington again."

"It is all real, and if you are able, which I suppose you are, to help yourself, and choose to go through that small door-way into the next room, you will find some very different clothing from that which you are now wearing. Put on the suit, you will see them by the fire, and then come out to me. You will, I think, find them fit you very well."

The boy appeared to want no second bidding: an instinctive aversion to the charity suit that he wore, induced him to get rid of it as soon as possible, and in a much less time than the lady could have thought it possible for him to make the change in, he came out so completely metamorphosed, that she could not have known him had she not have been in expectation of him, and felt sure there was no one else there.

He now looked a handsome lad, and somehow or another the whole bearing of the boy was different. With his workhouse apparel he seemed to have cast off the slough of a vulgar nature.

"You are changed," she said, "much changed; and now remember you are to answer to the name of William Black, and no other. Let what questions may be asked of you, you are to answer none of them, and you will consider me as your friend, Mrs. Black. Do you understand all that?"

"Oh, yes," said the boy, "perfectly; William Black I am to be, am I? I shall not forget that, madam, you may depend. But if people trouble me very much by asking me where I came from, what shall I say?"

"Say that you decline giving them any information."

The boy nodded his head, as much as to say—"That's quite conclusive," but he was a little annoyed to see the lady go into the adjoining room, and very carefully collect together his charity clothes, and place them in a drawer, which she locked up, as if the time might come when she should want them again—and that was really just what she was thinking of.

"Ma'am," he said, as he gently approached her, and laid his hand upon her arm, "ma'am, I want to speak to you."

"What is it? Say what you like."

"It is only this, that if you think you will ever send me back to the workhouse again, I would rather go at once; and then it will not be so hard to bear as when, perhaps, I am made used to something very different, you know."

"I have no intention to send you back."

"But the clothes—you are saving the clothes?"

"Yes, William, because it will be necessary for you to wear them once again, to oblige me, but not to go back to the workhouse. Rest assured of that, and if you comply with my commands without question or remark, you will have the means of becoming a gentleman, and need never visit the workhouse again."

"Ah, but I should like then to visit it."

"Indeed. And pray why would you like then to visit it?"

"Because I could go among the poor girls and boys, and at least make sure that they had, for once in their lives, a word or two of kindness spoken to them."

The lady arose from her seat and paced the apartment, muttering to herself in so low a tone that the only words he could catch distinctly were—

"I would rather have had him of a different temper than this. But no matter—no matter—the deep degradation and humiliation of a certain person will be fully felt before a discovery is made of what the boy is—who he is, is the grand question that will have its effect."

Suddenly then she turned to him, and said—

"This is a large house. You are free to go about it with very few exceptions. Never go lower than the hall, nor higher than the staircase above this flight which led you to these rooms, and do not leave the house on any account, unless you wish that the workhouse should again be your home, and continue to be so for the remainder of your life."

This threat was quite sufficient to induce the boy to promise a ready compliance, and that, too, a most candid one, in all her injunctions; so she left him to his own resources of amusement, seeming to care very little whether the time hung heavy upon his hands or not.

She seemed a strange, heartless woman, that; and yet any one who could have penetrated into the penetralia of her own room, where not even her waiting-maid was permitted to enter, would have been somewhat surprised to find her weeping as if she were the most feeling person in the world.

But these anomalous veins of human nature are common enough in real life. He that would see man as he is, must make up his mind to a thousand seeming inconsistencies.

As for the boy, he was, when alone, really much more amused than when his spirit of curiosity and research into all the wonders of that new abode, to him, was checked by the presence of her who, we suppose, from the solid advantages she has given to him, we may, for the present, at all events, call by the name of his benefactress; for certainly the change from Tippington workhouse to the superb house he was in, was very much in favour of the latter, which appeared to him to have endless charms.

Before, however, it occurred to him that he had had time to look about him, a servant, a young female, came to tell him that if he followed her she would take him to bed, as it was nearly midnight.

"To bed," said Twenty-two, "oh, I have had enough for to-night."

"Have you really? and yet you must come and have a little more, for it is Mrs. Black's orders, and I am not going to sit up all night because you don't want to go to bed; so come along with you at once, will you?"

There was a tolerable spice of asperity in the tone of voice in which this was uttered, and as Master Twenty-two was in a tolerable state of discipline, he made no further objections, but obeyed at once, and followed the servant from the room.

She led him up the staircase which conducted him to the limits of his powers of movement about the house, as prescribed by Mrs. Black; and when they reached a room in which there was a tolerable bed, she said with a sort of titter—

"I shall come for the light, young Master What's-your-name. Can you read?"

"Yes, a little; I can do a little of a good many things."

The girl left him, and he soon found out why he was asked if he could read, for John, the footman, had eased his mind of the load of indignation he felt by leaving the following couplet upon the dressing table—

"A ha'p'orth of bread, and a penn'orth of rats,
Is a very good dinner for charity brats."

"Ah," sighed little Twenty-two, "I have often envied the rats that used to run about in the workhouse, but if this is not all a dream, I shall not care what is said of me."

CHAPTER XXXI.

THE GRAND CONSULTATION AT THE WHEATSHEAF, AND THE DETERMINATION.

WE pity poor Booker, and yet there is something so comical in his distresses, that we cannot help laughing at him, and to be sure, as probably some of our lady readers will say, he brought it all on himself, that he did, for he ought to have made due enquiry concerning the Widow Mortimer before he married her, that he ought.

The idea of a man marrying her without knowing the number of husbands she had had before, it was really quite a piece of neglect, and as the lawyers say a man is always answerable for his own neglect—*laches* they call it.

But still poor Booker is not exactly to have the world's back turned upon him because he has not been altogether so prudent as you or I, reader.

And so thought Sherry, and his niece Amelia, and the young soldier, who came with quite a rush to the Wheatsheaf as soon as he could, having obtained leave of absence from his colonel, who, perhaps, thought such an indulgence was no more than he was entitled to, considering how much he had been pushed about, and how much he had suffered from the painful thought of how much more he had to suffer.

There was quite a grand consultation then held in the bar-parlour of the Wheatsheaf, at which Sheridan attended, and there were besides, Mr. Swanstone, a magistrate; Atterbury, the soldier; and Amelia, and even Maria came in now and then, and said a word, or offered a suggestion as it occurred to her.

Sheridan had duly detailed to the police the whole affair, and as Mrs. Booker had disappeared and was suspected to be rather a clever woman, the magistrate, Mr. Swanstone, thought that the less that was said about the affair in a public way the better it would be, and the greater chance there would be likewise of her capture.

Hence was it that the grand consultation was held, and it took place at the Wheatsheaf, as being much more handy for both Amelia and her uncle. Indeed the latter was scarcely in a fit state of mind to be moved about. His ideas were quite sufficiently bewildered where he was, poor man, and it was necessary that he should be a party to any plan that was adopted for the purpose of bringing Mrs. Booker to justice and to condign punishment, provided the evidence was really sufficient for that purpose, putting the ghosts of the five husbands quite out of the question, as creatures not likely to appear in a court of justice.

Mr. Booker sat in an arm-chair, with a look upon his face, as if he had but a very dim consciousness indeed of all that was going on; more like a man in a dream nobody could possibly look than did he.

"I fear," said Sheridan to Amelia, "that your poor uncle will be none the better for the explanations we now have to give him, and I almost doubt," he added, turning to the magistrate, "the prudence of making him a party to any of our plans—poor man—what do you think of it, sir?"

"I hardly know what to say."

"Nor I," said Amelia, "but yet he is very manageable by me, and at all events I think I may fairly enough take upon myself to say that if he is no great assistance, he ball be no hindrance."

"Then I am satisfied," said Sheridan, "so let us proceed to business at once, and I think, Mr. Swanstone, you said as we came along that you had a something to propose."

"I did, sir, and it is that the most absolute silence should be preserved concerning this affair, in order that Mrs. Booker, who, no doubt, is concealed somewhere not far off, may not take the alarm, and preclude all possibility of our catching her. From what you have told me now, I rather think she cannot be exactly aware of whether or not you dropped some of the poison upon the cut finger of Mr. Booker, before you took away the green bottle with its horrible contents, and in that case she will expect the death of Mr. Booker."

"I begin to understand you, sir."

"I was sure you would very shortly, and if it be made out that Mr. Booker is dead, some one, you may depend, will make the attempt to claim the money of the Life Assurance Office, and so we may get a clue to the place of concealment of the lady."

"Do you think she would run so much risk even for such a sum of money?"

"I do—because she could manage it all by agency, you perceive, and it strikes me that we may lay a very pretty plot for her in that way."

"But," said Amelia, "you all of you seem to forget that Mrs. Booker was really prevented from poisoning my uncle, so that she will hardly believe in his death; and even then, if you by such a means succeed in finding her out, what kind of charge can be brought against her?"

Sheridan looked at the magistrate, who, for a moment or two, was silent, and then he said—

"Not a charge of murder, but the law takes cognizance of such bare-faced attempts at murder, although I am far from being prepared to say but that she would get off from want of evidence of a guilty knowledge of the poisonous contents of the green bottle."

"Then, in point of fact," said Sheridan, "the whole case is beset with the most unusual difficulties."

"Well," said Mr. Swanstone, as he rubbed his nose with the end of his spectacles, "perhaps it is; but still I should recommend that Mr. Booker should pretend to die, just to see what Mrs. Booker would do upon that circumstance. It is an event which will bring her out in some way, you may depend."

"We will speak to him about it," said Amelia; and then leaning forward, she addressed Mr. Booker, saying—

"Uncle—uncle—do you comprehend what is going on?"

"Eh? Oh, yes. Perhaps he will be better after his brandy-and-water," said Mr. Booker.

"What does he mean by that," said the magistrate.

"Oh, he is continually saying it," replied Amelia, "that is, when he speaks at all. It seems to have been the last sentence that made a tangible impression upon his brain."

Sheridan nodded in acquiescence.

"Dear me," said Mr. Swanstone, "that is very singular indeed. But, however, I should advise that he be persuaded to pretend to be dead. It will be quite easy for you, miss, and the young woman in the bar, to keep up that sort of delusion for a few days, which will, I think, be quite sufficient to enable us to find out the retreat of Mrs. Booker, and she can be indicted for endeavouring to administer poison with a malicious intent. You see, the grand thing will be to get her in some way or another convicted of felony, in which case the crown will become legally possessed of all her property, and Mr. Booker will get back that foolish deed by which he has bound himself as it appears to keep up the life policy premiums."

"That, indeed," said Amelia, "would be a good object."

"Then I am willing to act in the matter," said Sheridan. "Amelia, you explain it to your uncle the best way you can, if you please, and remember we will leave this to you to manage with all the tact you can. I presume, Mr. Swanstone, you will have the death of Mr. Booker noticed in the papers."

"Yes, oh yes. You may leave that to me quite safely, sir; and now I think we need not intrude upon this family any further. Good evening, Mr. Booker."

"Oh! ah, to be sure," said Booker.

The magistrate shook his head, as much as to say, that he considered Mr. Booker's wits were terribly wool-gathering, and so indeed they were; but after bidding Amelia good night, and getting out into the street, Sheridan turned with vivacity towards the magistrate and said—

"Sir, you have some other reason stronger than any you have yet stated, for wishing Mr. Booker to simulate being dead. Is it not so?"

"Mr. Sheridan, it would be an insult to your penetration, to say it was not so," replied the magistrate.

"Ah! I guessed as much. Is it a secret from all the world?"

"Yes, with one or two exceptions, and one of those exceptions is yourself, so that now we have no listeners, I will tell you what will surprise you very much indeed, and let you see that my belief in the probability of capturing Mrs. Booker, when she thinks that Mr. Booker is dead, but not before, is based upon tolerable grounds."

The magistrate then entered into a statement, which did not take long to tell, but which certainly surprised Sheridan not a little. What that statement was, it would be premature on our parts as faithful historians to tell just at present, inasmuch as having the whole of the facts before us, we happen to know that such a matter will come out more explanatory and effectively a little further on.

Let it suffice that Sheridan was satisfied, and he said—

"By all means, then, let it be so, and I certainly think with you, that much is to be expected from the knowledge of the supposed death of Mr. Booker reaching the ears of the lady."

"I am glad we agree in opinion," said Mr. Swanstone. "and I would advise that the matter should be presented in that light even to Amelia, for with all her good sense and discretion she might, from some latent feeling of womanly compassion, be worked upon to thwart us."

"I do not think that."

"Well, well, it is best to be safe."

"Certainly, and as the secret is yours, and I have promised to keep it, you may depend upon my doing so to the utmost. I only hope things will be so timed, that you-know-who will not be irrecoverably caught in the noose."

"Oh, depend upon me for that. He shall be in danger, and no more. Now, therefore, Mr. Sheridan, I have the honour of bidding you good day, and I will send to you, you may depend, so that you may be present at the finale of this affair."

"I should be amazingly sorry to miss it," said Sheridan, "and besides, there is another person whom you know of, and who has no small amount of curiosity regarding the business. Indeed I am expressly commissioned to let him know when there shall be a likelihood of any *denouement* of an interesting nature, in order that he may be present at it. You understand."

"Incog., of course?"

"Oh yes, yes. Therefore, you will be pleased, Mr. Swanstone, not to recognise anybody of that description."

"Rely upon me; I understand perfectly what is required, you may be assured I shall not forget it."

"The plot certainly thickens," said Sheridan to himself, as he walked towards Pall Mall, "and how it will end, Heaven only knows. It is a strange affair from first to last. But of one thing I have somehow a suspicion, and that is, that Mrs. Booker is not the sort of person to be so easily outwitted as my friend Swanstone seems to think. By Heaven, she is a wonderful woman. What a pity it is that honesty and high principle are so rarely allied to high talents, for that she possesses the latter, no one can doubt."

"Alas! for human nature, that such a remark should be capable of being made by one who was so good a judge of the world as Sheridan, and made too, with the most perfect truth, for no moral philosopher ever uttered an axiom of such stern reality, as that high talent by no means brought in its train high principle.

Mrs. Booker was a remarkable example of such a state of things, for no one can doubt her guilt, while certainly no one will doubt her fascinations and her ability.

CHAPTER XXXII.

LORD MARCHMONT HAS THE HAPPY DAY FIXED, AND IS AS MISERABLE AS POSSIBLE.

"PASS the wine! Pass the wine! Now for a bumper toast!" cried Colonel Hill, as he, Sherry, George, and Lord Marchmont sat together the following night in a private room at the Mitre.

"Well," said George, "what's the toast to be this time? Let us have something short and smart, and epigrammatic. But I think it's Hill's turn for a toast and sentiment—er—or is it Marchmont's?"

"It is Marchmont's," said Sheridan. "Now for it, let us have something uncommonly lively, Marchmont."

"Lively, did you say?"

"Yes to be sure, out with it."

"Well, well, if you must have it, I will give you a toast which has come uppermost in my mind only just now, but as it is consonant with my feelings, you shall have it. It's rather gloomy though."

"Never mind that, out with it."

"Bumpers then, gentlemen, bumpers, and the sentiment I give you is one I think that will provoke reflection. All I can say is, that it ought to do so. 'Our family vaults,' gentlemen, if you please."

"Our what?" cried George.

"Our family vaults."

"Confound your sentiment! what have we to do with our family vaults, I should like to know, till we take up our lodgings there. I never in all my life heard such an abominable toast. It's positively disgraceful, that it is. Our family vaults, indeed. I'll not drink it."

"Nor I!" cried Hill, "nor I."

"Suppose," said Sheridan, "we add something to it, and say, 'our family vaults and our ancestors, and may we never disturb them in possession, or obtrude upon them our company!'"

"That's better," said George, "but yet it has an ugly sound. What is it that makes Marchmont so lugubrious?"

"I have no objection to say," replied Marchmont, "that it is my approaching marriage with the usurer's daughter, of whom I told you. The more I think of it, the more full of despair I get, until there are times when I could blow my brains out with vexation. And all this evil has come upon me, merely because I owe a few thousands. Is it not enough to make a man wish himself in his family vault?"

"Look at the prince," whispered Sheridan.

"Ah, how abstracted he is—what is the matter with him—I never saw him look so thoughtful."

"Why the fact is, your last words have awakened what the novelist would call a sympathetic chord in his heart—you are aware, probably, that on a somewhat larger scale he is in precisely your situation, and the German princess whom he is asked to marry as the price of his debts being paid, is to him——"

"Wormwood," muttered the prince, suddenly—"pass the bottle, pass the bottle—come, my lads, drink away dull care, for if we don't kill it, it will kill us, for a certainty."

The prince drank with a kind of desperation, and Marchmont followed his example, so that he soon forgot his cares, although, when any chance word brought up anything connected with his marriage, he winced a little and changed countenance.

The carouse lasted till past midnight, and then the little party sallied out into the streets in search of amusement as they termed it but really for the purpose of indulging in freaks, which then were as popular among the young sprigs of fashion as a short time ago they were in London. Some knockers were wrenched off—watchmen assaulted—a sign-board or two dislodged, until finally Marchmont left the party, being near to his own lodgings; for notwithstanding the copiousness of his libations, the open air and exercise had recovered him sufficiently, to begin to feel again the force of his melancholy situation.

Stevens, his valet, was sitting up for him, nodding with sleep before a large fire ; and before his master retired to rest, he put into his hands a note, which ran as follows :—

"Gray's Inn.

"MY LORD.—My fair client, who is so shortly to become Lady Marchmont, has graciously consented to fix Tuesday as the day on which she will make you happy ; and she does so, because of the great and flattering impatience she is sure you feel, that an early day should be named.

"I have the honour to be, my lord,

"Your lordship's most obedient servant,

"JOHN BOYNE."

Lord Marchmont bit his lips, and muttered some words that certainly would not do to be repeated to ears polite, and then tossing the note upon his dressing-table, he said, "Good night,

No. 12.

Stevens," and at once retired to bed—yes, to bed, but not to sleep. It was Saturday then, and on Tuesday he was to purchase emancipation from debt at the price of his liberty, and perhaps of his peace, for ever—ay, perhaps, too, of his honour for all he knew, and he was tenacious of that.

Fatigue at length closed his eyes in slumber; but his imagination was awake, and peopled his dreams with horrible images, foremost amongst which was a horrible and monstrous looking hag, who was continually putting a ring upon his finger and telling him that she was Lady Marchmont, while a deep noisome and stagnant ditch seemed to be flowing between him and all his old associates, whom he saw gazing at him from a distance, with looks of compassion and dismay. Truly such slumbers were not likely to be very refreshing to my Lord Marchmont.

He was haunted, too, with the consciousness that it was incumbent upon him, the first thing in the morning, to send his assent to the proposal that had been made to him for the marriage coming off on the day mentioned to him in the attorney's note, and yet the more he thought of the matter, the more bitterly repugnant he became to it.

He rose in the morning with a head aching and a mind wavering most sadly. A fellow feeling, the poet says,

                    "Makes us wondrous kind;"

and now as Lord Marchmont saw a very lugubrious look upon the face of his valet, he asked him what was the matter, with more real kindliness than he had ever yet used towards him.

"Oh, sir," said the valet, " I am thinking of you."

" Hark ye, Stevens, I am more averse to this marriage than ever, and I will not wed a woman whom I have of course every reason in the world to believe is of low origin, and who at the same time I have not even had an opportunity of seeing. I will not marry her."

"That's all very well, my lord, but what's to become of us if we don't marry her, or somebody who will relieve us from our debts. There's the rub, you see. It's all very well to say what we won't do. The difficulty is to say what we will do, and something we must do."

"I am half distracted."

" And so am I, but yet, my lord, there may be a plan thought of; I have your interest so much at heart, that really the more I think of it the more inclined I am to give your lordship advice that may counteract the evil resulting from the marriage,"

"Say on, say on; any suggestion that presents to me a chance of release will be most welcome."

" Then," added Stevens, in quite a confidential tone, "then, my lord, what I have to say first, is in the form of a question, and it is, how and in what manner the ceremony of the marriage is to be conducted, and where ?"

"If an answer to those questions be essential to your plans, I can only regret, Stevens, that it is out of my power to give one. You know as much of the affair as I do. I have, as I told you, given a written promise of marriage, and I have had an interview—hang it, it cannot be called an interview with the lady—and then this note has come from Mr. What's-his-name, the attorney, fixing the day, and there I am."

" Well, my lord, I don't know that all that constitutes an insurmountable bar to my suggestion, which goes upon the notion that as the lady has thought proper to conduct the courtship in the dark she may, likewise, also conduct the marriage. Do you understand, my lord."

"Not exactly. You must be a little more explicit, if you please."

" Very well, my lord, I will. It seems to me that the lady has some very special reasons indeed why you should not see her before she becomes legally Lady Marchmont, and that therefore she will be married to you in the dark, and such being the case, I really see no reason why your lordship should not go through the ceremony by deputy. We can easily get some devil-may-care fellow to go through the ceremony, and at the end of it, when a light is thrown upon the business, your lordship can appear and get safe possession of all the documents which this lady promises to place in your hands in exchange for your name."

"Stevens," said Lord Marchmont, springing up, " you are the Heaven-born valet! It shall be so ! By craft we will meet craft, which surely is fair all the world over."

"Extremely fair, my lord."

" I will leave the details to you, Stevens. Find a person to play the part you propose. Neither you nor he shall fail in receiving an ample reward. By Heaven, I feel a new man at the prospect of being no longer yoked to such a dreadful alliance; I would not again pass through the sufferings of the last few days for a dukedom, Stevens."

" Very likely not, my lord, but remember that all the plot hangs upon the one fact of the marriage ceremony taking place in the dark."

"It does, it does; and it shall be so."

CHAPTER XXXIII.

THE MARRIAGE.—A DENOUEMENT.—MRS. BOOKER OUTWITS SOME PEOPLE.

"Now, uncle," said Amelia, "do you understand me. You are to pretend only to be dead. Pretend you know, and all that is required of you, is, that you should keep your chamber for some days. Do you comprehend all that, uncle?"

"Oh, yes, ah; perhaps he will be better after his brandy-and-water."

"It's hopeless," said Amelia, with a sigh. "It's quite hopeless, Maria. His mind is so much shattered, that it is quite hopeless, I fear."

"Well, Miss Amelia, I don't know that it so much matters, you see, for after all, a man who is to seem dead, has nothing to do, and so the less he does the better, don't you think so?"

"Yes, but the difficulty is, to get my poor uncle to do nothing."

"Well, Miss Amelia, just shut him up in his own room, and leave me to attend upon him. I'll warrant that nothing will go near him, for people ain't so fond of corpses as all that comes to, and if he don't make a great noise, he won't run any risk of being found out in a large house like this. I think it may be managed very well, Miss Amelia."

"I sincerely hope it may, for Mr. Sheridan and Mr. Swanstone both make such a point of this sham death business, that I am quite convinced they expect great and gratifying results from it, and they have far better reasons than they have explained to me."

"What, is there anything we don't know?"

"No doubt, there are a few things, Maria; but come, shut the shutters of the bed-room nearly, and go down stairs, and draw up some of the shutters below. Look as solemn as you can, and say that Mr. Booker is no more; Mr. Sheridan writes to tell me, that his death will be noticed in the newspapers of this morning, so you see we must be prepared."

"And what shall I say he died of, miss?"

"Oh, no one will ask you, and if they do, it is a very easy thing for you to say you don't know. Now, uncle, will you listen to me for a moment; uncle, I say."

"Oh, ah, yes, of course."

"I make a particular request of you, that you will not go out of this room or the next until I tell you. Do you understand that?"

Mr. Booker looked as if he had some faint glimmering of what she meant, and then muttered about being tolerably comfortable anywhere, and was going on to say that perhaps he would be better after his brandy-and-water, when Amelia, who from hearing him say so so often had quite a horror of the expression, left him abruptly, and herself went down stairs to superintend the partial closing of the house, so that at the first glance, any one should know old King Death had paid a visit to the establishment.

We must now, however, leave the Wheatsheaf, and all the parties connected with it, while we proceed to state what took place at the nuptuals of the eccentric lady who had formed so golden a plan to make herself Lady Marchmont.

Lord Marchmont was so elated with the plan of Stevens, his valet, for outwitting the usurer's daughter, that he sent him to Gray's-inn with the reply to the lawyer's letter, and with full instructions to use his own discretion in the conduction of the affair.

Of course, the first grand point was to find out if the lady really intended to be married in the dark, as well as courted under such circumstances; and if she did not, Lord Marchmont had made up his mind to dare all the consequences of refusing to ratify his share of the agreement.

Thus armed, then, as a diplomatist, Mr. Stevens took his master's note to Gray's-inn, and casting a disdainful look at Peter, he told him to say to Mr. Boyne that he, Mr. Stevens, waited in case any answer should be sent back to his lordship, and that he was empowered to arrange the affair for the noble bridegoom.

This was duly told to the attorney, who therefore had Mr. Stevens into his private room, when he said to him—

"Your master will fully understand that the personal incognito of the lady is to be kept up until after the ceremony of marriage."

This was just what Mr. Stevens wanted, but he put on a demure look, and said—

"I am quite sure his lordship will not like that mode of conducting the proceedings, but of course, I suppose, if it must be so, it must be; and pray how do you propose to arrange the matter?"

"Simply thus :—A special licence will be provided, and the parties can be married anywhere— say even here; or in any church, provided it be at night, that his lordship may suggest. I should, for my own part, say that it will be better in a church."

"So it will," said Mr. Stevens, after a pause of some few moments, during which he was thinking which would answer his purpose best. "A church, by all means. Now there is one at Notting-hill—a nice little church. What do you say to that, sir?"

"My instructions are to leave that entirely to his lordship. Let it be the church you mention—what is its name?"

"It is called St. Barnabas Church, and is situated——"

"Oh, I know it—I know it. You have only to tell his lordship to be there by nine o'clock on the evening of Tuesday next, and he will find his bride in readiness for him; and I shall be there to hand him the papers that it is understood are to be restored to his lordship upon that most auspicious occasion."

"Then, sir," said Mr. Stevens, rising, and scarcely able to conceal his satisfaction, "I may consider that my mission to you is over, and all I can say is, that I hope the union will be a mutually satisfactory one, and that Lord and Lady Marchmont will live together long and happily."

"Of course," said the lawyer, "I e ho that wish most sincerely; and I don't at all see why it should not be so."

"Oh, dear no, nor I—nor I; there can be no reason in the world. I have now the honour of bidding you good-day, sir. I hope to have the pleasure of often meeting with such a real gentleman."

With mutual bows, then, and mutual compliments, these two persons, who each looked upon the other with a degree of suspicion that would have effectually prevented them ever being real friends, parted.

*   *   *   *   *   *

It is a cold night. There is a drizzling uncomfortable rain falling, and not a star peeps out from the black sky, to shed the tiniest reflected ray upon the dark earth. Stern necessity alone peoples the streets with rapid pedestrians. Those who have snug, cosy homes, and bright fires, and no engagement without, draw their easy chairs closer to the hearth, and listen contentedly to the splashing of the shot-like rain, and the occasional whirring howl of the wind in the chimney,

And yet this is the night on which the marriage of Lord Marchmont with the unknown lady was appointed to take place at the little church at Notting-hill. The clergyman was a young man, and a poor one; he was easily persuaded to indulge "the whim" of the parties to be married in the dark; he was told it was a family custom on the part of the noble bridegroom. It was of little real consequence, and he, as he looked upon the twenty-pound note that was placed in his hands, with a request that he would consider that his fee, consented.

To be sure, clergymen are human.

But nobody bargained for such a night as it was, and yet there it was, and there was no altering it; and in our capricious climate, a promise to marry when there was a fine evening would be a very doubtful affair indeed; so nobody thought of putting it off.

It wants twenty minutes to eight, and two men are standing beneath some trees in the immediate vicinity of the church. One of them is Stevens, the valet—the other, a stranger.

"Now," said Stevens, "you quite comprehend; you are to make all the proper responses, and to put the ring on the lady's finger. You are to leave the church at once; but, in case you should be wanted, wait am ng the grave-stones, and if your presence should become indispensable, you will hear me call to you. Do you understand all that, my friend?"

"Yes, master, it's quite understandable enough," said the man; "but I ain't paid, you know, for anything more than just the marriage. If I am to be called in again, or to wait even, I shall expect another five pounds."

"Which you shall have. The wish is, of course, to pay you as liberally as possible; you will have nothing to complain of on that score, my friend."

Among the tombs, and out of ear-shot of the valet and his friend, were three persons, and one of them whispered to the o hers, "I say, it requires no small amount of enthusiasm or of curiosity to be out on such a night as this. A plague on the whole affair."

"Hush, Mr. Sheridan," said one of the others, who was Mr. Swanstone the magistrate. "Hush, do not speak so loud; this is a most rascally night certainly, and I am wet through already. But hark! there goes the chimes of the three-quarters past seven; we have not long to wait, and the officer I have here will do his duty."

In the interior of the church are two old women, conversing, as they sat upon the steps leading to the communion table, in whispers, and lighted by a solitary looking candle, for none of the lamps in the sacred edifice are lit; and that very candle it is quite understood is to be taken away as soon as the bride arrives.

A carriage dashed up to the door of the church at three minutes before eight, and a lady got out and crossing the threshold rapidly darted into a pew. The carriage waited. Then a hackney-coach drove up and a gentleman alighted, and then another, followed by a lad—that other was Mr. Boyne, and the lad was Peter—arrived on foot. The solitary candle still burnet on the steps of the communion-table, while Lord Marchmont, in close talk with Stevens, entered the church; for Stevens had met him the moment he alighted from the hackney-coach in which he came.

"All's right, my lord. He is here."

"You are certain he is ready to take my place as soon as the ceremony begins?"

"Oh yes! He is now hidden in the churchwarden's pew."

"Thank Heaven, I shall yet escape, and get my bills and bonds too, which is a great matter. This is the biter bit with a vengeance, Stevens—hush."

One, two, three, four, five, six, seven, eight, struck the church clock, and one of the old women who was present took up the light, and walked hobbling away with it as the clergyman appeared though a side door in full costume for the occasion. What a pitchy darkness reigned in that place—a darkness of the most intense character. Truly the couple who were about t be united might be black, blue, or brown, for all they could possibly tell of each other. Lord Marchmont stood close to the rails at the top of the steps, and then suddenly some one was pushed past him, and Stevens whispered, "Come away—come away; your substitute is there. This way, this way."

Nobody had heard any female footsteps, but when the clergyman, who was of course only recognisable by the tone in which he spoke, said—

"Are the parties who are to be united in the holy bonds of wedlock present?" a female voice answered—

"I, the bride, am here."

"And I, the bridegroom!" Lord Marchmont heard some one say, and he thought the voice was a very tolerable imitation of his own, let it come from whom it might, for he knew nothing of the person procured by Stevens to play the part for him in the marriage that was being carried on under such extraordinary circumstances.

Now there was a death-like stillness of about half a minute's duration, after which the clergyman commenced the service, "Dearly beloved," &c. and the responses were given by both parties tolerably clear. There certainly was a little fumbling in the dark when it came to putting on the ring, but that essential part of the ceremony was at length satisfactorily accomplished.

"There is a good light in the vestry," said a voice, which Lord Marchmont at once recognised as that of Mr. Boyne the attorney, from whom he hoped and expected to receive the important papers, the possession of which was his great inducement to take all the trouble he had. With a start, his lordship turned rapidly, saying—

"Which way—which way? Amid this impenetrable darkness how can I find my way to any vestry."

Then came a gleam of light from a half open doorway, and small as was the ray that shot into the church, it was astonishing the effect it produced upon the whole place and upon everything in it. Lord Marchmont hurried forward, and he just saw a lady enveloped in ample drapery, and whose hands and face were covered with a large veil, precede him in the doorway. Then he ran against some one who begged his pardon, and he saw that it was Mr. Boyne with a small blue bag, which that gentleman tapped with his disengaged hand, significantly saying—

"The bills and mortgages, my lord, the bills and mortgages; they will all be in your possession soon. There is a capital fire in the vestry, and all I have to say is safe bind safe find—a word to the wise. I would throw them all in in a lump, my lord."

"Perhaps I may, but not before looking at them, you may depend, Mr. Boyne; I wish, and I intend, to be quite safe."

By the time this brief dialogue was over they had reached the vestry, which was a small ecclesiastical looking room, of an octagonal shape, and in which a good fire was burning, while a couple of wax lights blazed away upon the table that was in the centre of the apartment. A veiled lady, the one that Lord Marchmont had seen go before him through the small door, sat immoveably upon a seat. The clergyman was there—Stevens was there—Peter was there—and a getleman.

"Your lordship," said the clergyman, "will have to sign the register."

"Oh!" said Lord Marchmont, "I have no objection to give you my autograph. It seems a fine old church, although rather small, I imagine."

The clergyman looked puzzled, and when Lord Marchmont had written his name, he remarked that it was terribly in the wrong place—and so it was, for it did not appear to have the least connection with what else was on the same page of the book. Mr. Boyne, while the still veiled bride was taking off her glove to affix her signature to the register, handed him the bag of papers.   The most cursory examination convinced Lord Marchmont that they were right, and he did cast them into the blazing fire.

"So perish forty thousand pounds worth of debts," said the attorney.

"And so is my scheme of retribution I swore to him accomplished," said the bride, as flinging back her veil, she disclosed the features of the Widow Mortimer.   Lord Marchmont gave a groan, and staggered back as she added,—"Seven years ago, my lord, I fell a victim to your baseness; you deserted me, and I swore to you that I would have a revenge you little dreamt of.   I have forced you to marry me; there is my signature, Maria Booker.   I was the Widow Booker—I am Lady Marchmont."

"Hold!" said the strange gentleman, stepping forward, "you are my prisoner, madam, on a charge of attempting to poison your husband, and likewise there will be a charge of bigamy against you, Mrs. Booker."

The little door of the vestry was at this moment flung open, and Amelia Booker, accompanied by Sheridan, Master George, and several others, appeared.   Amelia was very pale, and she staggered to a seat, as she said—

"My uncle has been found dead in his bed!"

"Where's the charge of bigamy, then?" cried the Widow Mortimer, as we had better call her.   "I am Lady Marchmont."

"No," cried Lord Marchmont, with vivacity, "you are not.   In the dark it was another, and not I, who married you.   You have met the reward of your own treachery, and my bills and notes are a mass of white ashes, thank God!"

The widow rallied again.

"Indeed," she said, "then you have met with the reward of your own treachery, for the bills and notes you had, and have destroyed, were only copies.   You will find *our* child in a coach at the door—a charity-boy!"

Here Lord Marchmont staggered back as if he had been shot.

"Seize her!" he said; "she at all events tried to murder her husband, Booker.   Sheridan had the poison analyzed."

"Hold!" she replied.   "I know all about that.   Mr. Griffiths, the chemist, in St. James's-street, analyzed it; but there were two green bottles in the cupboard, and Mr. Sheridan took what was poison for flies, and left the harmless embrocation.   Now, what have you got to say against me, any of you?   Let any one here, at his peril, lay a hand upon me."

"Stop her—stop her!" cried Lord Marchmont.   "Stop her!"

It was in vain; she had, when they all least expected it, darted out of the vestry; and although the most vigilant search was made for her, and the hottest pursuit instituted, no tidings could be got of her.   She was never heard of from that day to this.   But Lord Marchmont had to fly to the continent to escape his debts.

     *   *   *   *   *   *   *

Upon a *post mortum* examination of Mr. Booker, it was proved by some eminent chemists that he had died of poison, and it was conjectured that she had found some means of administering to him a deadly poison, that she knew would finish his existence in time to prevent him from being a bar to her union with Lord Marchmont.

The house at Pimlico was shut up, for the story soon got wind.   Amelia married Tom Atterbery, the soldier, on the same day that Maria married his friend, the drummer.   It was long before Sheridan and the Prince ceased to talk of the Widow Mortimer, and the strange circumstances connected with the fate of the seven husbands she certainly had got rid of, and who were firmly believed to haunt the great bed-room of the old deserted tavern.

THE END

LONDON: Printed and Published by E. LLOYD, 12, Salisbury-square, Fleet-street.